Tony Cornberg is 27 years
upon Tyne where he work_ __ _ _____.__ __ ___-
employed criminal and immigration practice. He is
also Director of the Institute of Private Tutors which
undertakes enhanced Criminal Record vetting for those
involved in one-on-one tuition with children and
vulnerable adults; a company whose creation was
motivated by the same chilling events that inspired
Unnoticed.

TONY CORNBERG

UNNOTICED

Copyright © 2005 Tony Cornberg

The moral right of the author has been asserted.

Apart from any fair dealing for the purposes of research or private study, or criticism or review, as permitted under the Copyright, Designs and Patents Act 1988, this publication may only be reproduced, stored or transmitted, in any form or by any means, with the prior permission in writing of the publishers, or in the case of reprographic reproduction in accordance with the terms of licences issued by the Copyright Licensing Agency. Enquiries concerning reproduction outside those terms should be sent to the publishers.

Matador
9 De Montfort Mews
Leicester LE1 7FW, UK
Tel: (+44) 116 255 9311 / 9312
Email: books@troubador.co.uk
Web: www.troubador.co.uk/matador

SUFFOLK COUNTY	
LIBRARIES & HERITAGE	
H J	05/10/2005
F	£6.99

ISBN 1 905237-15-4

Cover illustration: © Photos.com

Typeset in 11pt Plantin Light by Troubador Publishing Ltd, Leicester, UK
Printed in the UK by The Cromwell Press Ltd, Trowbridge, Wilts, UK

Matador is an imprint of Troubador Publishing Ltd

*For my parents and my sister, Christina,
for a life filled with support and encouragement.*

For anyone Unnoticed who can't bear to be watched.

ONE

A pause. He slowly rose to his feet as he had done countless times before. Silently he breathed in as his eyes rose to meet those of the witness. It gave the impression that he was gearing up to attack the witness but in truth it was a habit he had not yet broken since the nervous days that he started the job.

"I shall be brief," he said. Another pause.

The Judge had made it clear that he felt this witness' oral evidence unnecessary. Maybe it was. There was nothing particularly contentious from his statement. But here he was, a result of the error of whoever it was that had covered the preliminary hearing. And he *had* to say something in his evidence that either added to, or detracted from, his statement, otherwise there would be trouble because there would be no real reason to have him here in Court at all.

So what the hell can I get him to say? In situations like these there is only one thing to do. Gamble – look like a genius or an idiot. Take a massive risk that may well have an impact on the life of a Defendant. An impact on your reputation. Everyone will be watching. What if it goes wrong? But then, what choice do you have? No use just thinking about it. You will have to take the gamble. So here goes.

"When you arrived at the scene and spoke to Mr Walton did you at any time ask him… let's say… what size shoe he took?"

Oh God this really is a gamble. Where on earth did that come from?!

A puzzled look came over the witness' face. His brow

tensed up as he looked nervously to the Judge and Prosecutor as if seeking confirmation as to whether or not this was a joke. No joke. Not in this kind of case. A man was dead. A driver was charged with causing the death by dangerous driving.

"Constable?"

Where the hell was he going with this? He had heard about Simon Silver before and the way that he caught you out. The way he operated in such an unpredictable fashion that either made him look like he didn't belong in the profession or that he was so adept at it that you were actually in the presence of genius.

"Er, no. No, I didn't."

"Thank you. Did you ask him at any time what his favourite colour was?"

"Well, no…" replied PC Watkins, still puzzled.

There was a silence and the Officer, already a little wound-up, broke it.

"Er, look I don't really see where this is going," he replied with his palms raised in the air towards Simon, seeming apologetic but in fact angry.

"Indulge me."

"No. I didn't ask him that. I didn't ask him any of those things."

"Constable, did Mr Walton *tell* you any of those things?"

Crown Court. All very official. He's obviously up to something. I have no idea what. Slowly, gently, fall into his trap. Even though you know that's exactly what's happening.

"No – he didn't tell me, Mr Silver."

"And why do you think that is?"

PC Watkins looked at Simon and said, patronisingly, "I suppose that would be because I didn't ask him wouldn't it?"

"Indeed." A pause to look at the Jury.

"Might I refer you to page two, paragraph eight of your

statement?"

The Usher passed a copy of PC Watkins' statement to him.

"Found it?"

"Hold on...yes, here, I have it."

"Read it out please."

" 'Mr Walton could not explain what had had caused the fatal collision'."

"Pause there please. Be careful when you answer this question. Why was it that he couldn't explain to you what had caused the collision?"

Silence. Golden, at least potentially.

" I know where you are going with this. I *did* ask him to explain."

"Then please be kind enough to explain to the Court why there is nothing to that effect in your statement."

Silence. Fidgeting. Palms previously raised in hidden anger were now beginning to sweat.

"I'm not trying to get at you Constable, you do a good job."

"Maybe I didn't ask him. I can't remember exactly."

Another opportunity to look over at the Jury duly seized by Counsel for the Defendant. Simon had, in all honesty, never thought he would get such a favourable answer. Now the Officer was on the ropes. And when that happens you just have to keep throwing punches.

"And yet you seemed sure that you *had* asked him a moment ago."

Trap closed. What a fool. As if someone would talk about their favourite colour after having been involved in a car accident! But the Officer hadn't thought to question it properly. He had assumed that he was simply being asked a ridiculous question. Simon knew he would do that. They always do. He had made the Officer think. And that's always the key to ruin a witness. They aren't there to think. They are there to know. Or to say that they don't know. That's all. Make a witness think and you have them.

The Courtroom is a funny place. People often use words they would never use in real life. They behave differently too. Nerves can do that to you, make you act differently. It's easier for advocates of course. They just have to ask the questions. But every witness, professional or otherwise, has a difficult job to do. They have one attempt to make their point. And perhaps due to the nerves, the enormity of the circumstance, it is possible to rob a witness of the sense that they carry with them in their usual daily life. They assume you are going one way and you trap them by going another way. It's not difficult to do – but everyone else does it one way and Simon never follows the crowd.

The gamble was actually paying off. And while his line of questioning may have looked odd to begin with, it looked like mastery now. And from that, another idea popped into Simon's head.

"Constable, what kind of car was the deceased Mr Thomas driving?"

"A Nissan Bluebird 1.6 LX" replied Watkins almost proudly. At least he was accurate about something.

"I thought it was a 1.8"

PC Watkins looked down at his statement though he was not actually looking for anything in particular.

"Sorry, yes, a 1.8"

Every time.

"Which side of the steering wheel is the mechanism for operating the windscreen wipers on a Nissan Bluebird 1.8?"

"No idea."

That didn't sound good and the Constable knew it.

"Is the mechanism for switching on the lights part of the

same mechanism which allows the driver to operate the dipped and full-beam functions on a Nissan Bluebird 1.8?"

"I'm sorry, can you repeat that?"

He did. To the letter. And without looking down at his papers.

"To be honest I don't know."

"So I take it that this was not part of your investigation, given that you may or may not have asked the Defendant to explain the cause of the accident?"

PC Watkins' heart quickened significantly as his brow joined his palms in sweating.

"OK that wasn't part of my investigation."

"So Constable, you had no idea what the cause of the accident was from the Defendant's point of view, since you can't remember asking him. And yet you did not investigate the workings of the deceased Mr Thomas' car, correct?"

"Yes."

Oh come on, put up more of a fight than that!

"So it is entirely possible, is it not, that the mechanism for switching the lights from full to dipped is on the same lever as for turning the lights on and off?"

"Yes, it is possible."

"Had Mr Thomas had the car for a long time or was it new?"

"It wasn't a new car – they've stopped making them."

"But was it new to Mr Thomas – had he just bought it?"

"I don't know."

"So he may well have?"

"I suppose so."

"Thank you. So taking this all together is it possible that what actually happened that night was that Mr Thomas, driving a car that was unfamiliar to him at night with his full beams on, saw a car approaching him and in trying to switch his lights to dipped inadvertently turned them off and became effectively invisible to the Defendant?"

"I can't say you are wrong. That might have happened. I don't know."

"Or could it be that he in fact used the wrong stick, turned on the windscreen wipers and while he flustered in trying to turn them off took his eyes off the road and drove into the Defendant's car?"

"I suppose these are all possible."

"But you can't say I'm wrong can you?"

"No."

There we go. Two reasonable doubts. From the Officer in charge of the case. And you only really need one reasonable doubt.

"Thank you Constable."

Thank you very much in fact.

The trial continued until the end of the day. The Jury took only 17 minutes to acquit the Defendant. That was Simon's record so far. He even got a respectful smile from PC Watkins as he left the building later on. Another successful day. Now he could prepare for tomorrow.

TWO

"Stop ganging up on me!" he said with a smile. Daniel and Hannah knew he was about to give in from the smile on his face and the fact that he looked like he was about to get up from his chair.

"Actually, I suppose we do need a few things for the week," said Paul, looking at his wife. He looked back at the children. "Alright come on then. But just one each ok?"

He walked out of the living room into the hallway to look for his shoes and rolled his eyes at his wife in a playful way, as though admitting that despite their children being a little bit spoiled he would still always give them what they wanted for just being cute.

They never had trouble in getting their way with him when they acted together. There was something magical about it when they did. Two people who he and his wife had created on separate occasions who not only got on with each other, but worked together. Paul and his brothers had been exactly the same. They knew exactly how to get round their parents too. Maybe he was such a soft touch with Daniel and Hannah because they reminded him of the time when he saw his brothers every day and thought nothing of it. Now they were lucky to see each other at Christmas.

It was as though he was rewarding them for being close. Siblings are often far from close. The notion of rewarding them was more comfortable to Paul than the idea of him giving in to them just because he was a soft touch, but in truth he knew that he was exactly that when it came to his children – the day that they were born he gave up his own life and prepared himself to concentrate on theirs.

Julie got out of her chair too and ushered Daniel and Hannah out of the room.

"Go on then – go and get your shoes!"

They raced upstairs, Daniel pleased to have been the winner, though by a small margin.

"Hey can you get a video on the way back?" Julie shouted through to Paul.

"OK," Paul replied. "Oh – hang on, you've got the card." He tied his shoes.

"Oh yeah, it's in the kitchen." Julie went to get the card while Paul got his car keys from the cupboard by the stairs. Daniel came down the stairs a little too quickly for Paul's liking. The look of faux-disappointment on his face told them he wasn't happy. In truth he knew that they were just excited but he felt obliged to say "Hey – now I've told you both not to run down the stairs. You'll not get any toys if you fall and hurt yourselves – they don't sell them in hospitals".

They didn't say anything, probably because Paul had not done his fatherly duty in such a patronising way as his own father used to do. Julie walked into the hall with the video card which she passed to Paul who turned to open the front door.

"Kiss!" she said.

Paul turned back, smiled at Julie and walked towards her. He put his hand on her cheek and they both closed their eyes as he pressed his lips gently against hers.

"Urgh – Daddy!" the children shouted almost in unison. Paul and Julie laughed quietly to each other. Julie looked down at Hannah.

"What are you taking your dolly for? You're only going to the shops. Leave her here," she said as she put out her hand to take Hannah's doll. Hannah wrapped her arms around her doll and swung her body away from her mother.

"Oh honestly, I don't know," said Julie, "well just don't lose her."

Hannah took Paul's hand in an extra display of defiance to her mother and Julie watched the three of them leave the house and get into the car.

THREE

That afternoon the three men went to St Mary's Primary School. At least, they parked outside it. They don't tend to allow cars past school gates anymore. They couldn't remember whether or not they had been there before – it didn't look particularly familiar. Maybe there were some new buildings since the last time. Even if they had been there, it wouldn't have been this year. They rarely went to the same place twice in the same year. They were very conscious of the fact that they might be seen and reported. That would mean at the very least buying a new car between the three of them which was even more of a problem now that they were three and not four. They had never been able to come up with a plausible explanation as to why they were parked up outside a school if it ever came to them being asked. There really is no explanation other than the truth. So they countered this by being vigilant.

It was always the same. A red-faced man drove the car. An older man sat in the back seat carrying a digital camera and a larger man who sat in the passenger seat carried a videocamera. This never changed from place to place. It allowed them a sense of routine and this was essential to their remaining unseen. It kept things the same. The red-faced man could look behind him. The larger man could look to the left. The older man could look to the right. It's what they were used to now.

St Mary's Primary school finished dead on three o'clock. They knew this because the red-faced man had found out quite by accident. He had been in a shop and was watching two children as they talked. Their mothers must have been friends though the children did not go to the same school. They argued over which school was better as their mothers flicked through magazines. Their way of assessing which was the better school was quite endearing to the red-faced man. How long they had for playtime. Where they went for school trips. How early they finished. The red-faced man was taking this all in as he pretended to sift through the birthday cards.

The three men found that children of the age that interested them rarely walk home on their own these days and if they do it meant that they lived very locally. Sometimes teachers would only let children leave the school if they saw that one or both of their parents was waiting for them outside. Or a childminder perhaps. Sometimes the men had been lucky though. This was no such day, however, and they settled for photographs and video footage. St Mary's was not a good place to park and they did not stay for long. But they did stay long enough to get several photographs of around 20 girls aged between four and seven.

The youngest children always seem to come out first and that meant that the group could get what they saw as the better photographs first and didn't have to stay parked up for too long. There were no nerves. There was no excitement. I was just a matter of amassing pictures and film for the men to collate and share later so that they could be used by each of the men when they went back to their respective homes.

FOUR

They were just driving back. It was nothing more than coincidence. The larger man had asked the red-faced man to drive to Benson's simply because he wanted to buy some cigarettes. The supermarket was on his way home. As disturbingly simple as that. He waited in a queue and produced a five pound note from his pocket to make his purchase. And as he waited for his change he looked around. He saw a man with two children walk into the supermarket. A boy and a girl. He watched them enter the main body of the store and on the strength of that he decided he would have a look around the store himself. Perhaps browse around the toys aisle, looking, in case anyone asked, for a toy to buy one of his children. He didn't have children.

No-one thought it odd. No-one even noticed him. And after a while the family seemed not to be coming to look at toys. So the larger man decided to leave. He would have bought a toy, just to look like he belonged where he was, but he felt no need to spend any money, such was his invisibility.

He passed the magazine aisle on his empty-handed way out. He passed the family, the children who he had been waiting to watch. They seemed to be arguing about something and it irritated him that he had been denied his opportunity to watch them for such a reason. The boy wanted two comics and his father was telling him he had to choose between them.

The little girl was standing patiently with her magazine in one hand and a doll in the other.

"Daniel – come on, just pick one will you?" said Paul

"I like them both!"

Paul was getting irritated now, his daughter's patience clearly not inherited from him.

"Daniel it's one or neither – now come on, Hannah's waiting to go."

The larger man heard her name. Now he felt closer to her.

Daniel threw both comics on the floor and stormed off. Paul, with one eye on Daniel and the other on the mess he had made, bent down and placed the comics back on the shelf. He took Hannah's hand and walked towards the grocery aisle.

The larger man kept walking. And when he got back to the car he told the red-faced man to find a space near the door. He told them about the little girl and her wayward brother. They wanted to see her too.

They waited. And it wasn't long before the family walked out.

"There," said the larger man.

They were just going to watch her. Nothing more. But this changed the moment Daniel decided to play the fool.

His father was carrying four shopping bags, Hannah was carrying her doll and Daniel was carrying nothing. As they approached their car, Daniel ran up to Hannah and made a grab for her doll. He snatched it from her hand and ran off, laughing. Paul looked unsurprised and called out to Daniel wearily to come back. He didn't – he ran on. And the red-faced man started his engine.

The car crawled up behind the family as Paul put down the shopping beside the car and ran after Daniel. The larger man got out of the car and walked ahead – the red-faced man drove on slowly. Hannah was waiting beside Paul's car, crying for her doll, at the annoyance and injustice of Daniel taking it from her.

Paul was now a decent distance from Hannah who stood patiently crying by the car, waiting for her doll to be returned to her. She didn't see who was behind her. The larger man walked at a fair pace towards her and caught up to her. He picked her up confidently with his right arm and began to run towards the car. She screamed.

FIVE

Paul heard Hannah scream and for a brief moment he wondered to himself why it was that he had picked this particular scream out, since she was screaming anyway. But something made him stop and turn around – this scream was somehow different. A scream that alerted her need for help rather than screams based on the injustice of what Daniel had done. Paul didn't realise it at the time but Daniel had stopped running too. He had been constantly looking over his shoulder as he ran away, to see how much nearer his father was to catching him – how much longer the game could go on. He ran no further when he saw Hannah being carried off by a man that neither of them knew.

Daniel froze. Paul did not. He ran towards his daughter, neglecting Daniel this time. He was shouting but his words were not intelligible – mere sounds, as though something primal would warn the man not to continue with what he was obviously doing. What was obviously happening. Hannah was being kidnapped. A word which now had personal meaning. No longer a word that Paul only heard on the news but a nightmare he had not prepared himself for. It was happening. He was watching it happen. To his daughter. No warning shot – this was happening right now.

There is something that brought human beings to the peak of the animal kingdom. Something we don't really think about as being too important. Something that we possess that other animals tend not to, or at least not in such abundance. We are used to it now, so much so that we don't notice it, we only comment on situations that display a lack of it. We refer to it as common sense and while there are many things that distinguish us from other organic entities in a scientific sense, every human being has an instinctive common sense that allows us to think and react quickly. It sounds strange to comment on it such is our acceptance of its existence – it is something of a given and requires no investigation. But it was common sense that made Paul look on to where the man was running, carrying Hannah screaming and kicking. He realised that he was not going to catch the man now and he also realised that every second that he lost gave him less of a chance of getting his daughter back. Getting her back. Like he was accepting that she was gone now even though he could still see her. It was this common sense, and perhaps it truly is a sense, that made him shout out to Daniel.

Even Daniel, at six, had it. When his father screamed out "Daniel! Get in the car!" he knew that he absolutely had to do it. Like he would be slowing matters down if he didn't. He ran, carrying Hannah's doll by the arm, as fast as he could to the car and got in. Paul was running back to the car too and started the engine as soon as he got inside. He would put his seatbelt on while driving – he told himself that this would save him potentially crucial seconds. If only he had parked his car facing outwards he would not have had to reverse out of the parking space. How could he have known that his life and the life of his daughter were going to be altered forever by having unconsciously chosen not to reverse into the parking space? It was a vital factor in the equation as he would come to realise. Because as he reversed out, making sure it was safe to do so, he lost sight of the car with the men who had taken Hannah with them. He knew that there was only one way out of the car park and so sped towards it. He thanked God, though he didn't really believe in God, that he had not needed to stop for people at the three pedestrian crossings on the way to the exit. But it made no difference. At the exit to the main road there was a roundabout. The three men, though Paul did not realise that there were three of them at the time, could have gone either way.

What if he had kept running? Maybe he could have caught up. Since he didn't know for sure he began to believe he could have caught up. He thought to himself that perhaps he was, at that second, driving through what would have been the site where he caught up to the car on foot and saved Hannah. He could almost see it and looked in his rear view mirror to complete the imagining and make himself feel guilty. The process of Paul blaming his own foolish choice began at that roundabout. It had not been a foolish choice – it had made sense at the time. But Paul would always wonder.

Paul had a second to decide. Right or left? There was no-one behind him and Paul was pleased that he wouldn't inconvenience anyone while he made his choice. Why should he worry about that? It is perhaps another product of a civilised existence. There is no logic in thinking this way, yet we do. And his choice to turn left was also totally without logic. It just seemed to be the right choice. For absolutely no reason at all.

Paul was comfortable with his choice. He would never really know for sure but it actually was the right choice. The men had also turned left. In the dark-coloured car they were driving. What kind of dark-coloured car? It now dawned on Paul that he had absolutely no idea. It had looked like a people-carrier of sorts. It was. But there are so many of them. Taxis, cars for people who were also taking their children to the supermarket. Was it black? It could have been dark blue. Paul began to shake. In the moment he had not taken enough notice, so sure had he been that he would catch up with the car and never let it out of his sight. His common sense had not extended to perfection. Perhaps he would later forgive himself for this – accept his imperfections and hide behind them. After all, it is our lack of perfection that keeps us vibrant, organic and prone to emotion. Paul showed emotion now. His face was boiling hot, his palms sweating. He was crying. He was beaten.

Paul drove on at speed for a few minutes but realised that there was nothing more that he could do. She was gone. They, whoever they were, had her now. He slowed down and doubled back at the next roundabout. He headed back to the car park. He imagined that Hannah might still be there waiting for him, crying until she got her doll back. He even looked for her as he drove back to the space he had previously occupied. She was not there. This was no game. It had actually happened to him. Something that happens only to other people. His life was now defined by it. One day he would be eighty years old and talk about a kidnap that happened fifty years ago. He would tell people about it but while they would sympathise they would not take it as a warning of any kind. He leant over the steering wheel and broke down.

Daniel was too bewildered to cry but he knew not to say anything. He didn't understand what had happened but he knew at least that Hannah had been taken and that neither she nor her father wanted it to happen. He wasn't blaming himself. He had only been messing around. He would have given Hannah her doll back eventually, his father had caught up with him to such an extent that the game was almost over anyway. A few more seconds and he would have been caught and forced to return Hannah's doll. Adults rule children's lives. They know exactly what they are doing. Daniel felt no guilt – this was his father's fault and not his.

Paul didn't blame Daniel either. He blamed only himself. He didn't know what he could have done differently and whether, if he had done so, it would have made any difference. Perhaps the way he had managed the situation had led him to being so close to catching up to the car as any other imaginable possibility would have. Maybe he was just not meant to catch the car. Maybe he was meant to lose Hannah today. But he knew one thing he would have done differently – he would have chased Daniel but told Hannah to get into the car as he did so. She could have done too – the doors were open since he had been about to load the shopping into the boot. He hoped Julie would not realise this, see him as the unwitting victim that he was. Julie. Paul now realised that he had to tell her what had happened.

Maybe he could give it a little longer. Maybe it would be better to call the Police. They might catch the car and get Hannah back, then Julie would never need to know about it. Come on Paul, how could she never know? He would have to tell her. Hannah might tell her. Daniel might tell her. She would find out. He would have to tell her. But then telling the Police did make sense – the matter was still live. There was logically a good chance that the car might be caught; the faster he told the Police, the more speedy the response. Maybe it would also serve as a practice run for Paul – to hear himself actually say the words. Perhaps that would make telling Julie a little easier.

Paul picked up his mobile phone and out of habit checked to see if he had any messages or missed calls. This made him suddenly nervous – he had been gone a while – Julie might call at any time to see where he was – what would he say then? He dialled 999 quickly to avoid what would be an impossible conversation.

"Which service please?"

"Police." A pause.

A woman's voice came back "Northumbria Police" with an inflection that was not so much a question as an invitation to Paul to start talking.

"Hello?" said Paul, flustered, "it's my daughter. She's been," he started to pant, "taken."

"You'll have to slow down. Taken by whom?"

"I don't know! Someone just grabbed her and then, like, drove off with her."

"Where was this please?"

"It's the car park at Benson's"

"The supermarket?"

"Yes – they snatched her and they've just, like, driven off with her."

"Can you describe who took her?" The woman's calmness seemed to increase the more flustered Paul got.

"Not really. Look they drove off literally just five minutes ago, can you not just send a car to see if they can find them? Please?"

"Not without a description sir, there are lots of cars on the road."

There was no need for that. He knew there were lots of cars on the road. But now was a time for efficiency, not debate.

"It's a dark people-carrier. Black or blue."

"Do you know which way they went? I know that supermarket you see – which was did they go at the roundabout?"

A pause. This line of inquiry was going to go nowhere.

"No."

"Then did you at least get the vehicle's registration number?"

Paul's voice went quieter, he realised that he had failed in every way now.

"No I'm sorry I didn't"

Another pause.

"Sir there is very little a patrol car can do without information"

"Come on! It's a dark people-carrier – they'll be able to find it!"

"Sir, please, it would be impossible. Stay where you are and I will send a car there. You can make a statement and I will send out a message to all patrol cars to be on the lookout for a dark people-carrier in the area."

Why can't they just close the roads? They would catch them easily! Then they could open the roads again and everything would be back to normal. Science fiction Paul, you are just one man. You don't matter. Individuals may sympathise with you but they don't want to get home late and keep their families waiting.

Paul gave his details to the woman at the 999 call centre and waited. He knew it was no longer an emergency as such – the car would arrive but at normal speed. That meant waiting. That meant ringing Julie before she rang him.

Paul wondered what Julie would be doing when he rang. She would probably be sitting with a cup of coffee watching the television. She would hear the phone ring and get out of her chair. She would then probably walk over to the phone and laugh to herself, thinking something like "what has he forgotten to get?" or perhaps think he was ringing to make sure he had bought the right brand of something. She could tell when she picked up the phone, by the tone of his voice, that he was ringing for no such reason.

"Julie it's Paul," he said quietly.

That didn't sound right. He would never say his name – it would be obvious who he was, he would say something like "hi babe" or similar. She knew.

"What's the matter?"

"Julie they've taken her. Hannah's been taken."

She was going to ask him if he was sure. Had she definitely been taken? That was no kind of question to ask. Who had taken her? Why? What do you mean? When? Her silence asked all of these questions.

"The Police are on their way. They want to ask me for a statement. Julie I don't understand it. I just can't…understand…I'm so sorry."

Julie had not spoken since hearing the news.

"Julie?"

"I'm coming up there now," she said.

Julie's head felt as though it was being crushed by pressure from all sides. She felt hot all over. She was crying. She had to go to the supermarket. She had to see if what Paul said was true, if there was something that could be done. If there was a way out. She picked up the phone and dialled the number of a taxi firm.

"New Forth Taxis".

"How soon can I get a taxi from Gosforth?"

"About ten minutes".

"Right it's 17 The Beeches. Name's Julie Taylor." She put the phone back down.

She gathered her coat and even took her keys. She didn't need keys. Paul had keys. But it felt almost like she was on her own. She might need them. She put them into her coat pocket.

One minute. Two. Three. Why is it taking so long? Taxis only seem to drive fast when you are inside one – they seem to make no such effort when you are waiting for one. Maybe they had the address wrong. Maybe she should ring them back.

The taxi arrived just as Julie was considering this. It was actually early but Julie had been counting the seconds and it had felt like half an hour. She got in.

"Where to darlin'? You never said on the phone."

"Just to Benson's supermarket," she said softly.

He could see that she had been crying.

"Here what's the matter? Domestic?"

"Just drive your fucking car will you!" she shouted as she turned to look at the driver.

"Whoa – here, I was only asking!"

Silence. For the whole journey.

The journey felt long too. It was only a couple of miles.

She could see a Police car. She could see their car. This was real. She saw Paul talking to an officer and as they got nearer she saw a young female officer talking to Daniel, squatting down with her arm around him."

"Wonder what that's all about," said the driver

"Just here's fine"

Not much of a talker this one.

"4.60"

She handed him a five pound note and got out of the car.

"D'you want us to wait for you?" he asked but she did not answer, she just shut the door.

"Fuck y'then," he said as he drove away shaking his head.

Julie walked towards Daniel first. Partly because she didn't want to talk to Paul. Partly because she didn't want the female officer to comfort Daniel – that was for her to do.

The female officer stood up to face Julie.

"Mrs Taylor?" she asked as Julie walked past her.

Julie said "yes" very quietly and did not look at the officer as she did so. She bent down and picked Daniel up. She hadn't picked him up like this for almost three years. But he looked as helpless as he did then and made no fuss. It was getting cold. She put him down again and wrapped her coat around him. He had been keeping a lot of emotion inside him but he didn't need to do so now. He made very little sound as his face reddened and tears started to pour down his face. She took him to the car and sat him down inside. She joined him. He nestled into her and sobbed. She sobbed too now as she stroked his head. Nothing was said.

Paul was still outside of the car standing uncomfortably. He moved from side to side constantly. He scratched his head. He put both hands up to his face almost like he was praying. The male officer was taking a note in his pocketbook. The female officer was standing beside him. She felt a little redundant now that Julie was here but before long, their task complete, the officers got into their vehicle and drove away. They only spoke to Paul in the car park. It appeared that nobody else had seen a thing.

Paul climbed into the car but didn't start the engine. He turned in his seat to face his wife for the first time. She was his soulmate. His best friend. Yet he couldn't think of a thing to say to her. She broke the silence.

"Drive home Paul."

Without a word he did so, slowly and with care, as though this would make up for his failure in some way.

Julie walked into the house with Daniel and took him straight upstairs to his bedroom. Paul felt like a spare part. Julie had hardly even spoke to him yet. What should he do? Wait for her to come down? Go and see them both upstairs? Paul decided to get the shopping out of the boot instead. It needed doing sometime.

He made three trips to the car to carry in the bags, each time looking up to the second floor of the house to see if Daniel's light was off. He stocked up the fridge and cupboards and went to sit in the lounge where he stayed, listening out for creaking floorboards in the hope that Julie was coming downstairs. After a while he wondered again whether or not he should go upstairs. He felt like he needed to be invited to do so. He had received no such invitation. Maybe it was worse that he hadn't gone upstairs yet. Of course he should go up – why the hell was he sitting alone downstairs at a time like this? He climbed the stairs to find Daniel's light off and looked to his and Julie's room. The light was off there too. It was only 7 o'clock. He walked in and could make out Julie's body under the bedcovers. He walked over towards her ready to embrace her and be there for her. He would tell her that they would get through this, though in truth he didn't know how they would at all. He approached her almost nervously.

"Just sleep downstairs tonight," was all she said.

SIX

She had been trying her best not to cry for the whole journey. Something told her not to upset these people. She didn't want to annoy them. She cried almost silently, watching closely every breath that she took to make sure that it didn't make too much noise. It was hard to focus on doing this – it seemed unnatural. But she wouldn't be allowed to cry. They wouldn't like that. They seemed to prefer the silence – they didn't even speak to each other all that much. But they could see the tears in her eyes and this was enough for them. It was almost as though they were offended by the fact that she seemed not to want to be with them. The larger man shuffled in his seat. He began to get more and more restless. She saw this and reacted to it. He looked like he was about to erupt. His face was getting redder, he fidgeted, his hands being put constantly up to his head. He looked like he wanted to tear his hair out. The more she saw this the more it frightened her. The more she began to lose control of her focus. She was trying her best not to make noise, she really was. But it wasn't working. She was still irritating the larger man. She had to admit defeat and in doing so began to cry properly for the first time in two hours. The silence broken now, the larger man didn't even look at the red-faced man as he said calmly "pull over".

She was screaming now. The older man who was sitting beside her did nothing to try to settle her. It was as though it was not his place, as though the larger man was in charge and he had made a decision they would not question in ordering the car to be pulled over. She had trouble catching her breath she screamed so much. But she didn't move from where she was, as if she had accepted her position in the car and in the men's company, as though she was only objecting to it while not actually challenging it.

The car was pulled over to the side of the road at the next available lay-by and the larger man got out. He walked to the door that faced away from the road and opened it quickly, his hands shaking, leant over the older man and grabbed Hannah. She didn't feel it proper to struggle, her destiny controlled as it now was, and always had been, by adults. Although this did not stop her screaming. He lifted her out of the car, the older man's eyes following her as she passed over him. He did not move. His face gave away nothing of what he was thinking. Perhaps he was thinking nothing at all.

The larger man let Hannah down onto the ground and for a moment she thought that perhaps they were going to let her go. Maybe she had irritated him so much that he would just leave her and drive away with the men. Or maybe he was going to hurt her. Two conflicting extreme emotions flying round in her head made her cry more. And he didn't let her go. He grabbed the tops of both of her arms and held them so tightly that the pain was like nothing she had ever experienced. She spluttered. The tears were choking her. He turned her to face the road. Why was he doing this? What is he going to do? Hannah thought for a moment that he might push her into the road. But still he held her, more and more tightly. She cried uncontrollably. Why was no-one here to help her? Why was no-one looking? She fought for vision through her streaming eyes.

The larger man loosened his grip on her right arm and as he stood behind her he stretched out his right arm and pointed to the passing cars. She could see his hand stretched out past her right cheek. He shook her repeatedly.

"Look! They just keep driving!"

She cried more.

"No-one will help you! They don't care about you!"

He began to shake her arms more violently as his voice reached screaming point too. She felt his saliva splash against her face as he screamed.

"They don't stop! They don't even see you! No-one is even looking! Nobody cares about you! You're all on your fucking own now!"

Time seemed to stop as she watched car after car pass by. What could she do now? How are you supposed to react at four years old when someone is telling you that your life is without value? This was her reality now. She knew this almost instinctively. Perhaps that's why after a while she stopped crying and was carried silently and without struggle back into the car. Perhaps that's why she didn't cry any more after that.

She settled back into her seat and closed her eyes. The silence continued as the car pulled away. She heard only the gentle humming of the engine and the sounds of overtaking cars as she began to drift into sleep, thinking not of where she was or who she was with anymore, but of how she had never heard an adult swear before.

She had now been placed into a new phase of her life. A new league. Her existence was now theirs to determine – her reality theirs to command and control. She felt certain that she would never see her parents or brother again.

To the three men she was just another child. A number in a list that would get longer and longer as time passed. She didn't matter at all. And as she sat there in the car where many children had sat before she felt the older man kiss her forehead and fell slowly asleep.

★ ★ ★

Neither of the other two men had criticised the larger man for his actions at the roadside but he still felt that he might have taken a risk. He had perhaps risked exposing the group. The girl's disappearance would be on national news today and an appeal for witnesses would be made by some Detective who probably had children himself. This had happened before.

Perhaps some of the people in the passing cars would have seen her and thought it suspicious. They might report it to the Police and perhaps the men's route would be retraced. But they would not find her. The Police would only know the direction that the men had taken from Newcastle and while it would narrow the search they would never be able to track across every single country lane which characterised the area around the Calder Pit. The destination. That is why they went there. It isn't even on any maps any more. Even if they eventually did find her, she would have been buried under the house for some time once they worked out where to look. And then they would take time to sort out other issues – the kidnap in England, the killing in Scotland. The three men would have found a new place to take their children by then.

These thoughts jumped around in the larger man's head as he tried to mitigate his foolishness. But the real reason that he faced no criticism was the same reason he wasn't too worried – he was right. No-one had noticed at all. No-one ever does. They just go about their business being too English to think about wasting Police time with what must surely have been a baseless suspicion anyway. After all, it is beyond the imaginings of most people that crimes are committed in such a flagrant way, in the most ordinary of circumstances. This would be too harmful to their everyday life – no-one will accept that they are vulnerable to the whims of the nonchalant for the entirety of their life. But they are. That is what tells us that bad things happen only to the careless and when they do the circumstances are unusual. It would not have occurred to anyone who did see the larger man shaking Hannah that they were passing anything other than a girl being reprimanded for being naughty. Even though this took place at the side of a busy road. Too English to question the parenting styles of others. Hey we might need to stop for petrol soon. Did you see that programme about petrol station robberies the other night?

Such was the larger man's confidence that he too settled into his seat and closed his eyes, slipping comfortably into sleep.

SEVEN

Paul was totally bewildered. It was 7 o'clock. Just over two hours ago, Hannah had been snatched. It seemed like days ago, and yet it seemed like it had never happened. Like she was upstairs asleep like her brother. He went back outside to the car. He stood there for a few minutes, thinking about everything at the same time. He opened the door, reached in and picked up Hannah's doll. He walked back into the house and sat down, clutching the doll to his chest as Hannah had done earlier. He sat alone, his wife and son upstairs. He cried his eyes out.

He became very self-aware after a while. What if someone called? He thought about taking the phone off the hook. But then, how would the Police get in touch? He thought about who might be likely to ring him and decided that the best thing to do would be to ring them first.

Paul had three brothers. All older than him. He got on best with Darren, his eldest brother. And he needed him right now. He picked up the phone.

"Hello?"

"Darren it's me."

"Aalreet kid? What you up to?"

"Darren there's…there's some bad news."

"What is it? What's the matter? Is it mam?"

"No it's not mam – it's Hannah. She's been…she's been kidnapped."

Silence. Darren was stunned.

"Paul I'm coming round to yours."

"No – wait. I need you to ring Craig and Dean. And ring mam as well."

"Well ok – do Julie's parents know?"

Paul hadn't even thought about them. He pushed words out through more tears.

"No, I haven't spoken to them. Hang on Darren that's the door."

"Alright, put the phone down, I'll call round to Julie's mam and dad's"

"OK – then are you coming round?"

"Aye, we'll come round soon kid."

"Right, I'll see you when you get here."

There was another knock on the door. Really don't want visitors right now.

EIGHT

Jim Lowry had had a headache all day. Aspirin counteracted by numerous cups of coffee. And he even thought about going home early. But it's not for a Detective Inspector to do such a thing. He wasn't sure how much of it was down to his headache but today everyone had seemed more irritating than usual. Well, at least he hadn't been to Court today. That was a headache he had been spared.

This was week four of an Operation which had been launched to try to crack a gang of commercial burglars. So far they had names but no evidence. And he was bored. He had sent out twelve pairs of officers to carry out observations and they had been eluded at every turn. They came into the Station every so often with photographs of people talking to each other in cars or outside on the street. But there were no photographs of anyone actually carrying anything. So he had put them in a pile on the floor because they meant absolutely nothing. What he needed was a taped phone call. But no-one seemed to be using phones, cell-site analysis being effective these days. The gang knew that. All it takes is one gang to be convicted by phone evidence and from then on everyone gets scared. And they just talk to each other face to face instead, forcing phone analysis experts to start worrying about future income.

Someone knocked on his door.

"Yes??"

"Sir, we have some photos of Kirby"

Jim suspected Kirby to be number one in the gang. And so

for a moment he got excited.

"Are they any good?"

"Well, he's talking to a few of the others in the car park at the…"

"Put them on the pile," Jim said, sighing. He pointed to the floor where the pile was fast becoming a prominent feature of his office. The pile got a few sheets thicker and the officers both returned to where they were standing. Lowry looked up at them.

"And get out."

He loosened his tie.

Until a burglary actually took place, those photos were useless. And so far, all of the burglaries had occurred at places the gang had never been seen. Maybe they knew they were being watched. Probably. That wouldn't have surprised Lowry at all – the officers he had been assigned were incompetent at best. Except for one of them – Michael Austin. He was someone that Lowry knew quite well. He was a bright lad. In fact, he had pretty much come up with the list of names. So Lowry had him stay at the Station and direct the others. He could at least trust him, so much so that he was the only one whom he allowed to call him 'Jim'. Commercial burglaries. Lowry was wasted doing this.

He was not the only one who thought so. And when two Officers came back to the station to officially document a kidnap that had just taken place, the Detective Chief Superintendant called for Lowry to see her in her office.

"Ma'am?"

"Come in Jim," she said, "coffee?"

"No thanks," he replied. "Oh, go on then."

He took a seat, the only seat, by Helen Wilde's desk.

"You look done in!"

Lowry looked at the floor as Wilde stood behind him and

poured two cups of coffee. She placed his cup in front of him and sat on the edge of her desk.

"To be honest Ma'am I am done in."

"No luck with the Kirby investigation?"

Lowry laughed. Not with the tools at my disposal. And they *were* tools, mostly.

"Not really, just some photos of people talking. No evidence of what they are talking about of course, they could be meeting up to discuss Sartre's contribution to the world of existentialism for all we know."

Wilde returned Lowry's laugh.

"You never know!"

There was a pause. Lowry spoke next.

"So, yeah, nothing to tell you really. Is that what you wanted me here for?"

Wilde got up from her desk and sat down on her chair. Perhaps to look more official.

"No Jim, actually I am going to take you off the Kirby investigation."

"Thank fuck." He shuffled in his seat. "Sorry, ma'am."

Wilde let it go.

"Well, since you are obviously not devastated at the thought of that, have a look at this," she said, handing him the statement of Paul Taylor.

Lowry read it over and handed it back to Wilde with eyebrows raised.

"I do my shopping there," he said.

"Yes…I thought with you being local you might want to lead the investigation. You can have anyone you want to help you."

"Michael Austin," said Lowry without a thought, "and David Whelan – he's pretty keen so they say."

"Well, I'll leave that up to you. You've done a few of these before haven't you?"

Lowry was something of an expert with kidnaps, though he had never found anyone alive.

"I have ma'am, sorry to say."

"Ever done an appeal?"

That was one thing Lowry hadn't done. While he had experience, he had never been involved with an abduction investigation as a DI.

"No ma'am."

"Well I want you to do this one please. Do your tie up."

He did. She continued.

"First though, you'll need to go and see the Taylors, get a photo of the girl."

"OK – maybe a school uniform photo, they tend to get the public interested?"

"She hasn't started school yet Jim, she's only four."

Lowry was almost an old hand at this job, and he was only 38. But he felt a lump in his throat for the first time since he could remember. Four? He even felt his eyes well up as his headache thumped on.

Lowry felt guilty for swearing, for not taking the Kirby investigation seriously, even for having had his tie loosened. He didn't have any reason to feel guilty at all, yet he did. He had only just found out about the kidnap – it wasn't as though he was being unprofessional. But this was serious stuff now and he felt that his casual attitude so far would insult the family of this poor girl. A four year old girl snatched while her father's back had been turned for a matter of seconds. At least with the Kirby case there was an element of cops and robbers involved. It wasn't a serious case anyway. No-one gets hurt in cases like that. It may damage the pocket of the already wealthy owner of the factory, shop or warehouse, but there was no physical danger. And whenever the culprits were caught there was always a bit of banter with them. The Police didn't hate them. Sometimes they shared a joke with offenders like them. But not with people who abduct children. They were a different kind of offender, more sinister and certainly more cunning.

Kidnap was Lowry's principal revulsion because he knew what happened to the children. As an officer it was the thing that made him perform the most efficiently, inspired to do so through his own sense of odium. And he knew exactly what to do. He was going to catch this one. No matter what. He felt like four weeks of his life had been taken by Wilde having deployed him into irrelevance and monotony. And now she was returning his life to him. He was going to be out in the field again, feeling every moment. Getting involved, meeting a family and sharing their pain, easing it perhaps. If he found her. He was going to find her. And he wanted so desperately to find her alive. If only to prove it to himself that he could. Selfish perhaps, but the result would please everyone, even if the motive was not wholly philanthropic.

Lowry walked back down to his office and shouted "Mike!" as he walked past Michael Austin's desk. He did not look at Austin as he walked, beckoning to him to follow. He sat down at his desk and Austin faced him.

"Mike we've been taken off Kirby"

Austin pretended to care.

"Really? Why?"

"Because it's a waste of time for one thing. But the main reason is this."

Lowry handed Austin the statement he had read moments earlier. And Austin's face mirrored the way Lowry's had looked. He placed the sheets of paper carefully and deliberately back on Lowry's desk, treating them more gently than he usually would, perhaps a display of how he felt about the case. He was scared of it already. Scared of what he would find. But it excited him too. If they caught the kidnappers he knew how much it would mean to Jim Lowry – in the last twelve years there had been several unsolved disappearances and he had been involved in the investigation of all of them. But this time he would be leading the investigation for once. And that meant that compared to the last four weeks, this was going to be exhilarating, even if it was for the wrong reason.

"So what's happening with Kirby then?"

"I don't care"

"No, Jim, but what's happening with it? Are we all being taken off it?"

"Nope. Just me and thee. And I asked for you specifically so don't let me down."

Even though Lowry shouted him down quite a lot, disagreed with him openly and belittled him from time to time, Austin was right to feel pretty good about himself for having been hand-picked by his mentor. He wouldn't let him down. Lowry knew that anyway, he just liked to remind Austin who was in charge. It was not unknown for Austin to be a bit of a loose cannon every so often.

"Now first things first, Wilde wants me to put the appeal out on the telly. So we're going to need a decent photo of Hannah Taylor."

"Right, so we need to go round to the house then?"

"Yeah," he sighed, "you know, Mike, this bit never gets any easier."

★ ★ ★

PC David Whelan was a bit of a robot. He wasn't very popular. He was a nice enough guy in truth, but not while he wore the uniform. He was well known for creating paperwork for himself by reporting drivers for faulty brake lights, illegal registration plates and the like, and even more well-known for looking like he enjoyed writing the reports out. But ultimately, while perhaps disliked, everyone knew that he was *the* traffic cop. And that he was going to go places. Lowry was pretty much done with Austin now, he was already on the ladder. And so he decided to take Whelan under his wing too. But apart from that he quite fancied treating himself to a driver. Austin was a more than competent officer but his driving was an absolute disgrace.

It was Whelan's day off and he was going mad. Lowry phoned him at home and he answered it before it had time to ring twice.

"David?"

"Yes?"

"David, it's DI Lowry"

Whelan almost stood to attention. In his living room.

"Sir?"

"Look, son, I know it's your day off and all that, but I could do with your help on a new investigation."

"No – that's fine. Do you want me to come in?"

"No, no, we'll come to you. Just put your fancy dress on."

The line went dead. Lowry sounded like he was driving. Like he was already on his way round to Whelan's house. He was. It was presumptuous to be fair, but then on the other hand, this was Whelan they were talking about.

"I've not met Whelan before," said Austin as he sat in the passenger seat of Lowry's car.

"You won't have done. He's not really the socialising kind of bloke."

"Well, I have heard about him, actually. People talk about him quite a lot. You know, like in the canteen. It seems like they all take the piss when he's not there but apparently they're all shit-scared of him."

"I'm not surprised. He's going to outrank us all one day."

"What's he like?"

"He's alright. The reason he'll do well is that while he knows his stuff he also knows his place," Lowry paused, "you could learn a lot from him."

Always room for a dig at me, thought Austin.

"Then I will be sure to keep my eyes and ears open at all times, sir."

Lowry laughed. "you're a cheeky bugger, you are." He wouldn't admit it, but nowadays he considered Austin a friend. Not just someone he was friendly with, but a mate. Someone he could have a pint with. Well, maybe when he makes Detective Sergeant.

PC Whelan was waiting on the footpath when they arrived at his house. Lowry got out and Austin moved into the back seat. He knew his place too, when it was important.

Whelan approached the car.

"Very smart," said Lowry, as he handed him the keys to his car.

"Where are we going sir?"

"I'll tell you on the way."

Robotic was perhaps not a totally fair description of David Whelan. As he drove to 17 The Beeches, Lowry told him the story of the kidnap. He was disturbed by it but showed no more than compassion which humanised him at least a little.

"So what we're going to do is talk to this guy, Paul Taylor, and see if we can get a photo of the girl," Lowry went on.

"Is that for a press release sir?"

"Yes," Lowry replied. And then he thought about it. "Why the hell else would I want a photo of her??"

Maybe this kid was not all he was cracked up to be.

"Well, sir, you will have missed the evening edition of all

the local papers by now and so you'll only be able to put the photograph on the television. So I was going to suggest that you make sure you ask for one in gloss finish because they come out better on television screens."

Austin smiled. Ha! Up yours, Jim!

"Er, thanks David, I hadn't thought of that."

"No need to thank me sir, just doing my job."

This time Lowry smiled. What a nerd.

They arrived at the Taylors' house twenty minutes later. It was almost fully dark now.

"Right David, I don't want to overwhelm them cos it's getting late so if you don't mind, stay in the car."

Austin got out and walked up the path with Lowry.

"Mike – serious head on, right?"

"Yeah I know. I'm pretty nervous actually."

"So am I."

Lowry knocked on the door. Paul Taylor answered it. He had the look of a man feeling too many emotions for his body to handle. That was pretty much the case.

"Mr Taylor?"

"Yeah"

"Mr Taylor, I'm Detective Inspector Jim Lowry and this is DC Austin. Can we come in?"

Paul didn't look too surprised to see Police on his doorstep.

"Yeah, come in. My wife's upstairs in bed and so is our son, so we'll have to be quiet."

Lowry looked at Austin. And then turned to Paul.

"You should probably go and wake her up. She won't thank you for talking to us on your own."

"Well, she was at home when, you know, Hannah went missing."

"I know she was, but we need to talk to you about putting

an appeal out on the TV. And it will be better if you are all together."

Paul looked visibly nervous at the thought of an appeal. The door that had been opened when the larger man grabbed Hannah was leading to all sorts of places. He had seen appeals on the TV but in truth had never really paid much attention to them. Of course, he sympathised with the parents, especially when they cried, and he remembered the faces of the children, but he never imagined that he would be in the same position. He was. Right now. It was so real. And now new people had come to his house to remind him.

There was an awkward silence. Paul looked like he didn't know what to do. Like he needed to be pushed in the right direction. Austin felt so sorry for him.

"Tell you what Paul, why don't you go and wake up the missus and I'll put the kettle on?"

"Yeah. OK."

Paul climbed the stairs and Lowry followed Austin into the kitchen. Austin was ready to be chastised for taking the lead, but no slap on the wrist seemed to be coming his way. That was a good sign. As long as Lowry wasn't critical, Austin knew he was doing alright.

Paul almost crept into the bedroom. Though there was really no need, since he was going in with the sole purpose of waking Julie up anyway. He walked over to her.

"Julie," he almost whispered her name and she did not stir.

He sat down on the edge of the bed.

"Julie?"

A little louder this time.

She woke up with a start and for a moment thought there was good news.

"Julie, the Police are here."

"Oh. Right. I'll come down in a minute."

She got up and looked for a dressing gown.

"I said I'm coming, Paul. Just go downstairs will you?"

He deserved her coldness. At least he felt that he did as he walked downstairs again.

"She's coming down now. Go through to the living room and I'll bring the tea in."

Paul was so nervous that while he was preparing the drinks he couldn't remember how Julie took her tea. Maybe she didn't want any. He made some just in case and left it without sugar.

They sat in the living room, the four of them. And Lowry felt the need to speak first.

"You'll have to forgive me for being cold and clinical. But every second counts here. So I'm hoping you will both agree to putting the appeal out on the telly."

"Of course we will," said Julie for both her and her husband. "Do you want to do it here?"

Lowry hadn't thought of that. But she didn't need to know.

"Well, I didn't want to arrange anything without speaking to you first. But we can do if you want."

"Yes please," said Julie.

"OK – Michael, would you go outside and tell Whelan to arrange for the media to come here to the house? Both local news channels. And get the press as well – they can use the photo for tomorrow's papers."

"Yeah, 'course."

Austin left, giving Julie an understanding half-smile. Lowry went on.

"Right then, I need a couple of decent gloss photos of Hannah if you've got any. We can pick the best one for the news."

Julie had a photo in mind and so she went to find it, leaving Paul with Lowry.

Lowry could see his eyes were welling up. And the silence

was making it worse. While Lowry struggled to think of anything to say, Paul began to cry gently. He looked across at Lowry. Lowry seemed a good man to Paul. But he hated the fact that he had to be here. He hated himself and he felt hated too. He wiped his eyes. He controlled his tears, which wasn't easy.

"She absolutely hates me," he said

"No she doesn't Paul, she's dealing with it in her way."

Paul nodded in agreement, though he didn't agree.

"Seriously, Paul. Here, look at me. There's no right way to deal with this sort of thing. It's unnatural. No-one can prepare for it. I have seen it several times myself but I have no idea what it feels like, how you are feeling right now."

Paul let himself go again. Harder this time. So much so that Lowry got out of his chair and sat next to him. Paul took this as an invitation to lean into him and sob. He wasn't even embarrassed. Rightly so, perhaps.

Lowry knew this was no good.

"Paul," he whispered forcefully, "now you sit up straight. You've got a job to do here Paul and you have to look strong for your family. I'm not saying your wife needs looking after cos she seems like a fairly, well, strong-willed person. She obviously scares the shit out of you!"

Paul laughed through his streaming eyes.

"Aye…"

Lowry smiled.

"But seriously Paul, you can't lose it. You really mustn't lose it, right?"

Paul exhaled slowly a few times.

"Yeah…ok. I'm alright now."

"OK now here's my mobile number. Paul, it's my personal mobile right? Not my work one. Ring me any time you need either DC Austin or me. I don't usually give this out. But don't be shy about ringing ok?"

"Thanks"

He put it into his pocket. Lowry returned to his seat for when Julie came back, which she did soon afterwards, carrying a few photos of Hannah. At least she was sitting next to Paul. Austin's seat was empty now but she chose to sit with Paul. Though he probably wouldn't have taken it to mean anything.

Austin got into the passenger seat of Lowry's car.

"Alright?"

"How are the family?" asked Whelan.

"They seem to be ok, well, you know, as ok as they can be."

"Yeah."

"Anyway, we're going to do the appeal here at the house so we need to organise the press and TV crews so...do you know how to do that? cos I don't!"

"I think you just ring it in don't you? The station can sort it out I think."

"I have no idea. Seems like a plan though."

There was a procedure. But this would do for now.

★ ★ ★

It didn't take the various members of the media long to assemble at 17 The Beeches. Luckily, they had brought their own lights, which was a good thing because Lowry had not even thought about the fact that it was dark. Seems he had missed a few things today. And that headache was still letting its presence be felt.

He decided to call Helen Wilde before he missed anything else.

"Jim," she said as she picked up the telephone.

"Ma'am I just thought I would update you. We are about to put the appeal out – the media are all here."

"You're doing it at the house?"

"Yes. Is that alright?"

"It's fine – I think it will have more of an effect. Well done."

"Thank you."

That was a bit naughty. But no-one would know that it had been Julie's idea so he might as well take advantage of it.

"So is there anything specific you want me to say, or not say?"

"Actually, Jim, I'm glad you rang because there is something. In the statement you will find a few references to a black people-carrier vehicle."

"Yes I remember"

"Well I've thought about it and I don't want a load of people ringing up to report seeing a taxi do I? It inconveniences them and gives us false hope."

"But ma'am, what more is there to say? That leaves us with just a photo. Taxis are taxis ma'am – they all have lights on the roof. I'm sure people can differentiate."

"I know Jim but people sometimes get a bit excited when they are trying to help. Imagine what it will be like getting a lead and then see it come to nothing."

"Well, what can I say about the car?"

She sighed.

"OK you can say 'a dark vehicle'. But I don't consider that to be all that relevant anyway – the important thing is a description of the man who grabbed her and of course her photo. And what time it was. And where. Et cetera. If someone sees the girl then who cares about the car – do you see?"

"Fair enough. Ma'am, I should go and get the family ready for the cameras."

"Yes you do that Jim, keep me informed."

It made sense. And now he had to think of what to say to the cameras. But more than that, he had to tell Julie and Paul how to do something he had in fact never done himself.

★ ★ ★

"Inspector – can we get a picture of the girl?" shouted a reporter.

Shit.

"Yes – Mrs Taylor is gathering some photos right now."

Another reporter shouted out.

"Can we get the names of everyone who will be appearing for the appeal?"

Lowry signalled to Austin to deal with the reporters. He needed to speak to Julie and Paul.

Julie had done the best she could to make herself more presentable ready for the cameras. She had, after all, just been woken up. But she thought perhaps it would be better to look just like that. She handed Lowry some photos and he took them back outside, handing them to the reporter who had asked for them, though of course they would all be using them.

"Just pick whichever," he said and walked back inside.

"OK," he said to the couple, "I am going to talk first – giving the details. Fairly bland OK? Then you can talk to the cameras yourself, don't be afraid to show your emotions. The more emotional the better in a way. OK?"

Lowry was aware that he was saying "OK" a lot more than he usually did.

"And look, sorry this is so rushed, but the sooner this gets on the TV the better the chances are. Just be natural. Talk to them like you talk to me. Talk to whoever took her. Whatever comes out. It's not live so we can go again if need be."

Julie didn't seem too troubled by what she was about to do. Paul did, but then again Lowry thought that perhaps Julie would be doing the talking anyway.

They went outside to face the media, who stood in an arc in the driveway. Lights were hoisted up, neighbours looked out of their windows and nerves started to show. They tell you that when so many cameras are on you that it doesn't really matter which one you look at. And so Lowry decided to look at none of them. He would probably talk more freely if he could pretend that they weren't there. He began.

"At 4.50pm today Hannah Taylor was kidnapped by an unknown man in the car park of Benson's Supermarket in Newcastle-upon-Tyne. He made a grab for her and carried her off to a dark vehicle which was driven away at speed."

OK, doing well.

"He is described as being in his 40s, large build, wearing dark trousers and a blue sweatshirt. The driver of the vehicle was not seen…"

Paul's heart quickened. He should have seen the driver.

"…nor is there a registration number for the vehicle. We would urge anyone who saw anything suspicious at the supermarket tonight to call the incident room."

Done. But he had the easy job.

The cameras moved to Julie. She was stuck for words. How do you start something like this? Be natural, Lowry had said.

She breathed in.

"If anyone can…help the Police find my…our daughter…please…please call them. Even if it's something that didn't seem important. We don't have much…much description because everything happened so fast and…Paul tried to catch the man but he couldn't."

She paused as Paul put his arm around her.

"If…"

Now the tears started to fall freely.

"…if you have our daughter…please…we just want to

have her back. Please."

She started to sob. But there was one more thing that had occurred to her in that instant. It came from nowhere. Sometimes it pays not to prepare too well in advance. You lack the magic that spontaneity can sometimes afford you.

"Hannah...if you can see me, I love you."

It was absolutely heartbreaking.

* * *

It was on the radio at 8pm. And on the television news at 8.30. At 9 o'clock, in Durham prison, a man lay on his bed and his heart started to beat faster. At 10.30 he was smiling.

NINE

They had said very little up until the point of arrival and Hannah was still asleep as the red-faced man brought the car to a stop. The older man got out and lifted Hannah out of the back seat. She woke up slowly but didn't say a word. It was as though the fact that she was being carried meant that she had nothing to fear – she was not being made to walk. Maybe she was special after all. But then the larger man had shouted at her at the roadside – he said that she was anything but special. Then again, the larger man was not the one carrying her, the older man was. He had not shouted at Hannah, in fact he had not said anything at all. He had even kissed her gently on the forehead before she fell asleep – she could remember that – he felt bristly and while it made her forehead feel itchy she fell asleep soon afterwards and was not disturbed by it. Perhaps he would make sure that she was safe. Perhaps the larger man was just angry. Perhaps he was sorry and would apologise later. Sometimes adults do lose their temper, she thought, like daddy does. But he always says sorry afterwards.

Hannah had never known such silence. Even the wind made a sound and it wasn't blowing all that hard. She had never heard the phrase "in the middle of nowhere" before but she felt the same sensation as the person who coined that phrase must have done as she looked around. There were fields for miles, some with trees in them. There was a row of houses that looked as though they were a million years old. It was obvious that no-one lived in them. Some had no roof, many had no doors to speak of, weathered over time and probably rotted away. All except one. One that stood alone, away from the row though it was not bigger than the rest or special in any way. In fact it was a lot older than the others, though Hannah did not know this. It was the original house where a small band of pit workers lived during the week in the short time before the quarry had become profitable and led to the single house being joined by several others as more people were employed at the quarry together with new machines and technology. It had thrived for a year or so before the pit was exhausted and the workers moved on to either unemployment or a new job somewhere else.

Hannah could see the quarry now. It looked huge to her but in truth it was small by modern standards. It was reddish in colour and, as the sun was beginning to set, seemed all the more eerie. Hannah stared at it as the older man carried her up to the door of the house that stood alone and waited while the larger man, who must have gone in ahead while Hannah was being lifted out of the car, came to the door. He opened it towards himself and stood back to give the older man more room.

"Bring her in," said the larger man in a monotone voice, his arm outstretched pointing into the hallway of the house.

Hannah received no apology from the larger man. He had scarcely even looked at her as she was carried in past him and down some steps into a cold, dark room that smelled of hell. She had never seen the Calder Pit before but she seemed to cling to the memory of it now, perhaps because it was the last thing she had seen before being brought into the house. She began to wonder, after the older man placed her onto the floor of the cold room and walked out without a word, whether she might ever see it again.

TEN

"Boss!"

Eddie Dixon chose to ignore whoever was shouting.

"Boss!"

Dixon sighed. Let my first night on this wing be peaceful, please. At least give me that. Might as well go up – he'll only keep everyone awake.

Dixon climbed the stairs slowly. He still didn't know who was shouting.

"BOSS!"

He pursed his lips as he climbed the stairs.

"I'm coming! Stop shouting the place up!"

He shook his head though his disgust was not apparent to anyone other than himself, locked as they all were behind doors with no way of looking out.

He reached the source of the noise, though in truth it was something of a lucky guess. It could well have been the next cell.

He opened the hatch on the cell door just to be sure. Yes, there was someone standing up against the door trying to listen through it.

"Yes?" asked Dixon as though he was half asleep and already bored by a conversation that had not yet started.

"I have some information."

"Really?" he replied as though he didn't care. He didn't care.

"You sound a little tired. But you will have to wake up a bit

I'm afraid. Have you seen the news?"

"What?"

"The news. A little girly was kidnapped today."

Dixon was becoming more interested now.

"I know where she is, you know."

It was 10.30pm. Dixon was tired. His first ever shift on this wing finished at 11. Everyone else had gone to bed, whether they were asleep or not it didn't matter. The place was quiet. Ready for Dixon to have another cup of coffee and then go home. So this was not a good time for a windup. But then what if it wasn't a windup?

You aren't supposed to go into a cell on your own. Dixon knew this. And he knew why. But he did, if only to keep the wing quiet.

"Now you listen here," he said as he closed the cell door behind him and placed a hand on his baton, "I don't find you funny. I know what you are. And I don't care whether there is something wrong with you or not. All I know is don't take the piss. Not when I'm on."

Dixon was massive. And he was holding his baton. That made him someone who should be taken seriously, especially given his tone. But he was scaring no-one in this cell.

"I'm not trying to evoke laughter. I'm very serious."

His eyes did not flicker. He did not blink. He wasn't taking the piss and Dixon realised as much. And his heart quickened.

"The little girl from the car park?"

"Yes I want to talk to the Police. Detective Lowry, I believe, is the officer in charge."

There was a silence as Dixon stared blankly back. He must actually know.

"Don't waste time Mr Dixon. Go and use the telephone. I'll still be here when you get back."

Dixon released his grip from his baton. He no longer stood

so boldly as the little girl from the news appeared in his head. The photo of her smiling, dressed in a costume for what he thought must have been a fancy-dress party.

He couldn't be making this up. Why would he? He knew that if he was that people would find out and he would become unpopular, and being unpopular in prison was a state worse than being unpopular in a playground, whether it be in the eyes of the inmates or the officers. Dixon looked at him still. He had never seen him before now. For all he knew the inmate was a new arrival. He didn't know that he'd been there on remand for three months now.

Detective Inspector Lowry had finished work but he was still wearing his suit, even though he was at home and could be excused for having gone to bed. But there was no way he would sleep much at all tonight. The telephone rang only once before he picked it up. He took no convincing. Any lead would do right now – it would at the very least make him appear active and could of course actually point him to finding Hannah Taylor. He threw his jacket on and got into his car, driving straight round to DC Austin's flat, telephoning him on the way. Austin actually was asleep though he tried hard to sound like he hadn't been woken up. It was no testament to Lowry's skills as a Detective that he was not fooled by this – Austin sounded as though he actually *was* still asleep.

They arrived at HMP Durham soon after and Lowry parked the car while Austin went into the station nearby to pick up some tapes and recording equipment. They were ushered straight through the prison doors with the most cursory of security checks and were taken to meet the person who had called them. Dixon was visibly nervous. He didn't like the Police very much, as much because he thought they were corrupt as because he had failed to get into Northumbria Police himself.

"He's just through here," he said, pointing to a room along a poorly-lit corridor. "The Governor needs you to sign these though."

He passed them a document which Lowry didn't read, such was his excitement.

Dixon took them to the room and held the door open for them before following them in. But Austin turned to face him, scrunched up his nose and shook his head. Dixon took this to mean that they were happy to talk to the inmate on their own. He backed off, thinking that they were the Police and must know what they were doing. It did cross his mind to go and find a first-aid kit however. Just in case.

Austin plugged in the tape recorder as Lowry sat down to face the inmate.

"Ooh the Police. How exciting," he said with a smile.

Austin turned on the machine, put a tape in and pressed the record button.

"It's 11.34pm," said Lowry, "and we're in a conference room in HMP Durham. I'm DI 27759 Lowry currently stationed at Newcastle Central Police Office. Also present is…"

"DC 23553 Austin"

"This is an interview with, well, could you state your name for the tape?"

"William Hopper"

Lowry continued.

"Mr Hopper, we're here because we've been told that you've got something you want to talk to us about."

"Yes. I do hope I didn't get you out of bed."

"Don't worry – you didn't."

"Mind if I smoke?"

"No, go ahead"

"They're a bit funny about letting us smoke in these rooms you see."

Austin saw a chance to break the ice.

"The screws? What are they going to do, like? Put you in prison?!" Austin laughed. Alone.

Hopper lit a cigarette, inhaled and paused. He looked at Austin.

"I'll do the jokes," he said with a dead-pan face, "now don't waste your time with small-talk."

Lowry cut in.

"Right Mr Hopper what is it that you wanted to tell us?"

"The little girly on the news. Snatched at a car park eh? Risky. But by the speed you got here I would say that you are desperate for a lead."

He was right, but no-one confirmed as such.

"What do you know about the kidnap?"

"Everything."

★ ★ ★

Lowry looked at Austin. How could he know anything at all about the girl? The kidnap had happened only six hours ago. It had been all over the media. He could have just seen it on the television. Maybe he had. Lowry left Austin in the conference cell and closed the door behind him.

"Mr Dixon!"

Surely they weren't finished already? Had Hopper just been stringing them along? Dixon left the office at the end of the corridor and walked up to the conference cell. Only Lowry stood outside it.

"Mr Dixon I need you to help me with something."

"Yeah?"

"Has this man been out of his cell at all today?"

"Well…yes."

"Why?"

"Well this morning he would have been in the showers and then he would have been on association from 1 til 2."

"What about after 5?"

"No, he would have been in his cell from about 2 onwards."

"He *would have been*?"

"Well I only came on at 3 so I am just assuming. But they are always behind the door after association, unless they do education I suppose."

"You suppose. Does Hopper do education?"

Dixon looked pressured. He couldn't know everything. Come on, give me a break – I'm supposed to be finished my shift! This was a great first night on the beast wing. Dixon mumbled something which communicated the fact that he did not know the answer. Lowry looked at him calmly, though making him aware of the need for haste.

"Can you find out for me? Go and wake people up if you need to."

Lowry walked back into the conference cell. Hopper looked at him and watched as he sat back down.

"You don't look like you believe me," he said. He looked as though he didn't care either way. In fact, what's the point of convincing them anyway? Now isn't the time. All I need to do is give them a reason to believe me and then hold back.

"So – have you sent Mr Dixon to find things out about me? I could have saved you the time." He leant forward, "I've been in my cell all day listening to my radio."

"Then I don't believe you," said Lowry, gathering up his papers ready to leave.

Oh, don't go – there's a lot more to say yet. What more was there? The reason to make them believe him. True, he could have just heard things on the radio. Maybe they need to hear something that wasn't mentioned to the media.

"Sharan."

Lowry stopped.

"Now is that a lucky guess? Or do I know for certain what kind of car they used?"

Lowry thought for a moment. What had he released to the Press? He definitely hadn't said anything about the make of car – in fact, Paul Taylor's statement was silent on that. They had decided it was too risky even to describe it as a people-carrier – a lot of taxi drivers drive Sharans. It would have meant a lot of potentially useless calls from people seeing taxi drivers innocently doing their jobs. So they had decided not to mention the car in detail. It was a tough decision, but it seemed logical. So how did this man know?

"It was black by the way," continued Hopper.

"But Mr Hopper, that could be a lucky guess too. They only make them in green, black and silver."

Hopper's mind was ticking away now. If he could link himself to the car then they would know for certain that he was for real. Then he could take control of the situation and say nothing more until it served him best to do so.

"It could be couldn't it?"

Hopper smiled as he said this. As if he was admitting to having had a good shot but been caught out by people who were just too switched on, even at this time of night. Austin reached over to turn off the tape.

"Leave it on, please," said Hopper, "let's see how far I can push my luck. What if I was to tell you the registration number?"

Hopper had hoped it wouldn't go this far. That they would be desperate enough to believe him from the outset, perhaps by the very fact he had called them to the prison. It didn't really matter though – the men would have reached their destination by now. And the car would be well hidden. There was probably no danger in telling them the registration number – they would never know where to start looking for the car and it was a standard plate so no-one would have noticed it. The father of girly obviously hadn't.

"Let's see now. X…" he paused, as though the information was coming to him from a celestial source.

"X548 WZQ. How about that?"

"If you are making this up, I swear to God you will leave this prison in a fucking box."

"Well then, I had better hope that my luck holds for me. Now, you won't get a signal in here, so why don't you send your bitch outside to check the registration over the radio?"

Austin launched himself over the table and grabbed Hopper by the collar of his prison-issue shirt. Lowry almost had to prise him off.

"Look, we need to check the number ok?" he said to him quietly.

Austin gave Hopper a look which did not frighten him. He just licked his lips seductively at Austin and mouthed the word 'bitch' at him. Austin left the cell and Lowry followed him out so as not to tempt himself.

He waited outside the cell while Austin left the prison to allow himself a decent signal.

It took Austin longer to leave the prison than it did to run the PNC check and he soon came running back inside.

"You won't believe this," he said, catching his breath, "that car is registered to William Hopper."

Lowry would have been excited were it not for a niggling doubt he had. He never got too excited, only at the end of a case. When there was a conviction. Until that point things had a habit of going wrong or being argued out by PACE-happy defence Counsel.

"Hang on, think for a second," he said, and it was more

patronising than he had intended, "what's to say we haven't just got some pervert here who owns the same kind of car that whoever snatched the girl was driving? I mean, there are a lot of people-carriers these days."

Austin knew that Lowry might be right. Damn.

They both walked back into the cell.

"So?" asked Hopper, "did my luck hold?"

"I know what you're doing Hopper," said Lowry, "you have a black Sharan and you want us to believe that that links you to the kidnap."

"Why would I want to do that? You would charge me with conspiracy to kidnap! Why would I want you to do that?"

A good point. And neither officer could think of a reason why Hopper would want to do that.

"You see, officers, this is why to do your job you only have to be a certain height."

You don't have the intelligence to work out what I'm doing and that's why it will work.

"Not any more you don't Hopper."

"But you did when you joined up"

Another good point. Lowry allowed himself a smile despite the circumstances. He did enjoy banter even if it was with scum.

"So tell us more. You got us to come here. You obviously do know about the kidnap. What more can you tell us?"

"Only that I was involved."

"But you've been here on remand for three months haven't you? For taking dirty photographs?"

"Well done Officer! But I haven't been here forever have I?"

"What, so this was planned months ago?" It was taking a new turn now, it was more sinister.

"Maybe."

Not really.

"Don't piss about," said Austin.

Hopper's voice raised to surpass the volume of Austin's, "tighten his leash will you? He's starting to piss me off."

Now was the time to set the ball rolling – people were getting angry.

"Just tell us what you know," said Lowry, "then we'll leave."

"Why should I? Eh? You've been nothing but insolent since you came in. I want to go back to my cell now. Why should I help you? You're just rude, both of you."

Lowry's voice softened, testosterone being replaced by compassion for a little girl and her family.

"Because we need any help we can get. That little girl's family are in pieces. If you were involved then you can help save her."

Hopper folded his arms and looked away.

"No," he said, like a spoiled child.

Lowry did well to remind himself of his mandate.

"Please, Mr Hopper."

Hopper repeated Lowry's words in a childish voice and laughed.

Lowry turned off the tape. Now we're getting somewhere, thought Hopper. And quicker than I had expected.

"You're up at Court tomorrow aren't you?"

"Yes," replied Hopper, feigning fear.

Lowry waved the tape at Hopper.

"The CPS will love this. I'll make sure they add another Count to the indictment – conspiring to kidnap, just like you said. This little piss-take has backfired hasn't it?"

No. Far from it.

"You'll talk then I think."

That's right, I will. And on my own terms.

As Hopper sat waiting for Mr Dixon to escort him back to his cell he thought to himself. No going back now. They will add the charge. Now I will have more to answer in Court. This had better work or I'll be in here for the rest of my life.

ELEVEN

The smell of the cold room should have gone by now but it still lingered. It was powerful enough to make Hannah wince and shudder which she did, though this made no difference. It just got worse. It was so cold. The floor was made of concrete and had nothing covering it. Hannah sat cross-legged on it; she had found by now that it kept only a small part of her body cold if she sat like this. She could not feel her legs now – her lower body was so numb but she knew that if she lay down it would mean that she froze all over. She started to get irritated by her situation now. She had been given no explanation as to why she was in the cold room, in any room. In this house at all. But she checked herself and made no noise.

Her eyes were getting used to the darkness now, though there was in fact nothing to see. The room was completely empty. She was hungry. She had not eaten for several hours but only now started to notice it. She had no idea what time it was. It must be late. But she was so cold she couldn't sleep. She stood up, slowly to begin with, such was the numbness of her legs. Still there was silence, darkness and foul odour. Standing up had seemed to make it worse, as though she had disturbed the stagnant odour and made it swill around in the air and gain strength. The hunger pain worsened. She wanted to shout out to the men for food. But were they even still here? Would they hear her if they were? Maybe, but she didn't want to upset the larger man by making a fuss. Maybe they had just forgotten to give her something to eat. Sometimes adults do forget things, make mistakes.

After a while Hannah's silent benefactor, at least as far as she was concerned, came into the room. She had not heard him coming and had jumped with fright when she heard the key turning in the lock. She didn't know who it was and had thought it best to sit back down as she had been placed on arrival. The older man shone a torch at Hannah and walked towards her carrying some bread with marmalade thinly spread on it which he gave to her together with some juice that tasted as though it was as old as the house she was in. It didn't matter. She was too hungry to waste time by tasting anything. She was just grateful to have received the food. The older man was being so kind to her. He must have sensed her hunger. He must have known she would be hungry and had probably put a lot of thought into spreading marmalade onto her bread – he could have just buttered it, left it dry even. The older man knew that she would be grateful. They always are. And when she finished her meal he walked towards her as she stretched her arms out for him to pick her up and carried her upstairs to a room where the larger man and red-faced man were sitting.

They began to undress as the older man closed the door behind him. It was Hannah that broke the silence by screaming – the men stayed silent. No-one heard her screaming, partly because there was no-one for miles around the Calder Pit and partly because she didn't scream any more after the first time.

TWELVE

Lowry and Austin said nothing as they walked back to the car. But once inside Lowry looked at Austin. Austin thought he knew why and so spoke.

"Sorry about losing it, Jim."

Lowry laughed.

"Don't worry about it."

Was he being sarcastic? So far, Austin had never heard Lowry being sarcastic. He tended to be a fairly straight-talker. Lowry spoke again.

"God what a sick bastard he was eh? I nearly lost it myself."

The silence resumed.

"What's next then?" asked Austin.

"Well…I suppose we'd better give that tape recorder back. Then we can get it transcribed for in the morning."

"Transcribed? At this time of night?"

Lowry looked at Austin with raised eyebrows.

"Do you want to do it, like?" he asked, almost angrily.

"Well, no…but I mean, who's going to type it up tonight?"

Lowry looked away. And then he looked back. Austin smiled. They both knew who.

They returned the tape recorder and drove round to David Whelan's house. He was still up, but it wouldn't have mattered even if he was asleep. Lowry knocked on the door.

Whelan came downstairs in a questionable dressing gown and opened the door.

"Oh, hello sir."

"David."

They walked inside.

"David I have some news to tell you."

"Sir?"

"Mike – put the kettle on will you?"

Austin went into the kitchen.

"David, about an hour ago we got a call from Durham Prison. They said someone there had some information about Hannah Taylor."

"Sir?"

"So we have just been to see him. Hopper they call him. Anyway, he has confessed on this tape…" he gave Whelan the tape, "…to being involved in a conspiracy to snatch her. From prison. I don't believe him. So I need this tape transcribing ok?"

"Yes sir – I'll do it straight away. It shouldn't take too long."

"I don't doubt you David."

"I do have one question though sir."

"Go on."

"Well, sir, obviously it's urgent. But why do you need it if you don't believe him?"

"That's a fair question David. After all, you weren't in the prison with Mike and me. You don't know what this bastard is like. He's a fucking worm, David. A fucking worm. Anyway, he's up at Court tomorrow and I want them to add this conspiracy to the indictment he's facing."

"Did you arrest him sir?"

"No – why?"

"Well, don't you need to arrest him? Give him the chance to see a Solicitor?"

Austin walked into the hallway while the kettle boiled.

"Get your head out of the textbook David."

"Sir?"

"I do what I want. If the CPS don't like it I will arrest him tomorrow morning. With a transcribed interview to back me up."

"Oh right, I see sir."

"And stop calling me sir will you? My name's Jim," said Lowry as he walked into the lounge and sat down.

Austin smiled. Welcome to the club mate. You're going to love it. You're going to want to kill Lowry at least three times a day. But you're going to love it.

* * *

Austin sat down with Lowry in Whelan's lounge while their host fetched the tea.

"Er…Jim?" asked Whelan, nervously, as he passed him some tea.

"Thanks. Yes?"

"I was just thinking. If he's up at Court tomorrow, and he knows anything at all then it might be worth telling the family to turn up too."

"He's bullshitting, David."

"Maybe, but they should be told. Even just to show them you are following up on every lead."

It was a fair point. They were owed the courtesy at least.

"Alright, David, we'll tell the family. Good idea. But we'll finish this tea first. I need a few minutes before going round there again. That poor fella, Paul. He's a totally broken man."

Of course he was.

Whelan was already typing by the time Lowry had started the engine.

"He's a good lad, him," said Lowry

"Seems alright. And he calls you Jim now eh? Took me a

week before you let me call you Jim."

"Well Mike, the difference there is that you didn't say 'sir' every other word. God, by the end I wasn't even listening to him, I was just waiting for the next time he said 'sir'!"

Austin laughed.

"But apart from that, he has impressed me more than you did."

"Thanks."

Predictable. Lowry tended to decorate anything that even resembled a compliment with an insult. Austin was used to it. In fact he was so used to it that he hadn't wanted to kill Lowry at all today. Maybe it was time to put in for promotion.

They arrived at The Beeches within ten minutes. Newcastle is a small place when there's no traffic and they had driven almost from one end of the city to the other.

It was quiet there now. No cameras. No nosey neighbours. Most of the lights on the street out. There were lights on at number 17 though.

Lowry and Austin walked up the path and knocked on the door.

A larger, slightly beefier version of Paul opened the door.

"Who are you?" he asked.

"It's alright Darren, it's the Police," said Paul behind him.

"Oh, sorry lads, come in. Sorry."

They walked into the front room where seats were sparse.

"Officers, these are my brothers, mam, dad, Julie's mam, sister, dad," said Paul, pointing them all out.

"Hello everyone," said Lowry.

Even Daniel was there, although he had long since fallen asleep on his mother's lap.

Lowry told them what he had told Whelan. He told them that he didn't believe Hopper. But that didn't mean it wasn't worth them coming to Court. He told them that he had done a bit of digging around and found out that Hopper was in Court for taking indecent photographs of children. And that a man named Riley was prosecuting, so they should look out for him. He told them he would be there too, in case his instinct was wrong, which he hoped it would be. He told them it wasn't good news yet, that it was just news. But he would see them tomorrow, if they decided to go to Court. Of course they would go. Anything would do now, even if only to get out of the house.

THIRTEEN

Hannah woke up in the cold room where they had left her last night. She was trembling. It was freezing now. In fact it was the cold that made her wake up. She had no idea what had happened last night. Her first thoughts as she woke up were of the three men, wearing no clothes, in complete silence. Doing something to her that she did not understand. Each of them had done it, even the older man. Didn't they know that it hurt her? She was telling them that they were hurting her, by her screams. But they ignored her. They just continued. She stopped screaming after they had each done it once. Because when they each did it again, it was obvious that they didn't know just how much she wanted them to stop. It hurt so much, even now. Why were they hurting her?

She remembered how they had all put their clothes back on together afterwards, Hannah included. No-one said anything. The older man had then opened the door and took Hannah back downstairs. He put her on the floor gently. Why was he sometimes kind and yet twice he had hurt her in a way she couldn't explain? He kissed her forehead as he had done earlier on in the car. But this time he kissed her on the mouth too, just briefly. And he spoke.

"Sleep now, girly."

And then he left the room.

Now that she had remembered it all she began to feel scared. And she was not just troubled. She was panicking. She didn't think to try to escape, not that it would have done any good anyway. She sat trembling. Her eyes were still not used to the darkness in such a way as to allow her to see where she was. And she began to fear the darkness too. She felt around for the wall and when she found it she backed herself into a corner of the room. There was total silence. She joined her hands together around the tops of her legs, which she drew into her body. It kept her a little warmer. And maybe it made her look smaller so they might not see her, she thought.

A long time passed. In truth it was only an hour. And sounds came from behind the door. A key was turned. The red-faced man came inside with a torch. He shone it around and in the seconds before the light landed on her, she thought she had not been noticed. But soon she was and she began mumbling to herself and backing further into the corner. She knew it would do no good. The red-faced man walked over to her.

"Girly, come and play a game."

Hannah stayed where she was. She didn't want them to hurt her again. The red-faced man received no reply from her and so walked right up to her and knelt down. He took her and hugged her. Was he trying to say he was sorry? It might be alright. He could be forgiven, as long as her didn't hurt her again. He released her.

"Come and play a game with me, girly."

She followed the red-faced man upstairs. Into the room where she had been made to lie down the previous evening, when the hurting started. The two other men were not in the room. Hannah was alone with the red-faced man.

"They're asleep," he whispered, and put a finger up to his mouth to tell Hannah not to make noise.

It had occurred to the red-faced man that they didn't know Hannah's name. Not that they needed to know it for her sake, rather for their own. The kidnap would have made the news now and so they needed to know what she was called so that they could keep abreast of the news. They only had a radio at the Calder Pit – no television. And no means of buying a newspaper. So even though her photograph would have been released they wouldn't be able to follow the news without a name. They needed to keep an eye on the news. What if the Police had a lead on another kidnap but the men thought they were referring to this one? Then they would have to make a move back down to Newcastle, wasting perhaps several days that they could have spent with her. That would be a real waste of effort. They had driven a long way. Risked exposure in the car park and at the roadside, though past experience told them that the risk was minimal.

"So," he said quietly, "what's your name?"

Hannah had not spoken since she was in the supermarket yesterday. Her mouth had opened only to let out screams.

"Hannah," she said, looking at the floor.

"That's a lovely name," said the red-faced man.

She continued to stare at the floor, away from him. In silence.

"And how are you today Hannah?"

She felt like she was going to start crying again.

"I'm sore," she said.

"Aw…Well, that's just life I'm afraid," he said, turning now to look out of the window, "that's what happens. It'll go away soon though." He wanted to tell her she would get used to it, but he didn't want to risk her crying and wake the others up. They were tired. They had had a long day yesterday.

As it was, the larger man was awake anyway. He walked into the room half-naked and Hannah jumped when she saw him. He looked at her and said nothing. Then he looked away and carried on putting on the jumper he had carried into the room. He joined the red-faced man at the window.

"God what a lovely day it is."

"I know. Why can't we get weather like this at home?"

The larger man sighed in agreement.

"Oh by the way, girly's name is Hannah."

"Oh right. Hannah what?"

"Oh I forgot to ask!"

The red-faced man turned to Hannah again.

"Girly – what's your surname?"

Hannah didn't know what surname meant. The larger man grew impatient after only a few seconds. He walked over to her.

"What's your surname girly??"

She looked away.

"I…don't know"

She really didn't.

"You don't know?! You don't fucking know?! What do people call you? Hannah what? HANNAH WHAT?!"

She tried to shield herself from his shouting. And she cried now.

"Taylor," she said, too quietly.

"WHAT?!"

"Taylor," she said louder.

"Taylor. Right. Jesus fucking Christ! Simple enough question!" he shouted, as he turned away.

The red-faced man looked over at Hannah and smiled.

"A surname means your last name, girly."

When you are Hannah's age, you learn new things every day.

FOURTEEN

Simon Silver strolled into the Court building the next day. It was as though everyone knew about yesterday's trial. The papers had certainly been covering it. No-one said anything to him but he was sure they had heard. Simon only had one case today – just a Plea and Directions hearing and so once a plea had been entered Simon could spend the rest of the morning in the Advocates' lounge being patted on the back for yesterday.

He got into the lift and went upstairs. The Defendant today was a man called Hopper. He had apparently, so Simon's clerk had told him, asked for him personally. And riding on the back of that apparent seal of approval Simon had not bothered reading the papers yet.

He got out of the lift and walked into the Advocates' lounge and found a seat by an empty table. He didn't want to look like he was fishing for compliments. People could come and talk to him if they wanted to. He decided to look busy and so opened his brief for today and started to read it. Something struck him immediately.

He looked around to see if Alan Riley was in the room. He was prosecuting Simon today – the first time the two had met head-on. He wasn't there. Maybe he would be in the Robing Room. Simon got out of his seat and walked in. Riley was robing up.

"Alan," he said.

"Ah, Simon, hello."

"Alan I'm confused."

Alan Riley seemed to be more interested in tying his bands than listening to Simon.

There was a pause. Simon hadn't been faced with this sort of arrogance since he was a pupil.

"Why's that then?" asked Alan as he began to walk out of the door.

"Well when was this new Count added to the indictment?"

"Which case?"

"Hopper. You prosecute that don't you?"

"Oh yes, sorry – Hopper. Actually I need a word about that."

They walked up the corridor which afforded them a little more privacy.

"To be honest I'm not sure what's going on there either. He was originally charged with taking indecent photos and now that he is here to enter a plea for that they've added a new Count of Conspiracy to Abduct. Apparently it has to do with that girl that has been on the news – you probably saw it – Hannah Taylor she's called."

Simon had seen something on the news about Hannah Taylor.

"She was apparently snatched in a supermarket car park while her father was loading up the car. Bloody awful scenario really. Anyway they suspect he has something to do with that."

"But he's been on remand for a month Alan, how can he have been involved?!"

"Well this is the thing you see. They probably just want to guarantee a plea to the photos. They just added this to make him plead to that and then they'll probably just drop it – you know how it is. You should be over the moon anyway, you'll get the trial fee for a morning's work!"

Simon loved the job he did but he hated this part of it. The part where you give up just to cash in. That's not what the job is meant to be about. That's not why you study law and learn how to speak in public.

"Not interested. That Count goes Alan, it's totally improper."

"Not my decision my friend."

Friend? Let it go. Be professional.

"I'm not going to tell him to plead."

"Nor should you. But it will save you a lot of work! I'll leave it in your capable hands."

They are capable hands. Did you not hear about yesterday? With that Alan Riley walked back into the Advocates' lounge. Simon followed him but only to gather his papers. Now was probably a good time to go down to the cells and talk to this defendant. He couldn't see Caroline from his instructing Solicitor's office anywhere so he decided to go downstairs without her. She was perhaps in another Court. She would have heard about yesterday. Hopefully.

* * *

"Mr Silver," said Hopper with an arrogant confidence as he walked into the conference room where Simon had been waiting for about ten minutes. He carried a cup of tea in one hand and a cigarette in the other. He turned to face back into the corridor and signalled to one of the security staff with a quick jerk back of his head to beckon him over. He walked along the corridor to the room.

"Could you close this door for me please? I don't think I can turn the handle."

The security officer looked at Simon as if to ask why he couldn't have closed the door for his client. Simon was about to speak but Hopper spoke instead.

"Thank you very much indeed," he said in a way that

Simon thought was either patronising or so polite that this man was not the usual kind of punter.

"You put me in a spot there you know. He won't forget that. I would have closed the door for you if you'd asked."

Hopper smiled at Simon, dropped the cigarette he was holding, put his tea on the table and put out his right hand which Simon duly shook.

"I wouldn't want to put you in a spot," he said. And it would have appeared more genuine to Simon if Hopper hadn't held his gaze for longer than was comfortable.

"Have a seat please," said Simon holding out his left hand with an open palm. But Hopper was already in the process of sitting down.

"Now you know what today is about don't you?"

"Oh yes, I get to confirm my name and plead not guilty. Mind if I smoke?"

Simon answered the question with a wave of his hand though in truth he felt it wouldn't have made much of a difference.

"So it's a definite not guilty plea then?" asked Simon. Given the look on Hopper's face he knew the answer.

"I didn't expect to have to convince you," said Hopper in mock-disappointment. "I have heard such good things about you."

Simon was a polite man, patient and professional. But he was getting very close to acting out of character and it showed on his face.

"Right, look. I don't need convincing. I've got some extra news for you and it depends a great deal on how you are going to plead to the photographs. It's not the best news either."

"Oh this conspiracy charge? Yes I know. Awful."

"How did you know about that? I only just found out myself!"

"Only just got the papers did you?!" Hopper didn't care really. Not with what he had in store for Simon today.

Simon was a little embarrassed by this. Yes he had just got the papers but this is how the job works.

"It's perfectly normal to get briefed for a PDH and get the papers an hour beforehand."

Simon hoped that Hopper wouldn't know what PDH meant and this would allow him to sit back in the driving seat.

"Ooh, by the way, who was your pupil master? Who trained you?" asked Hopper.

WHAT? Why on earth is he asking that?

"Er, Donald Ramsey. Why?"

"Just curious. He's a red judge now isn't he?"

Great – he might as well have said 'don't try to trick me with jargon. I probably know more than you do'.

"Anyway, they've added this charge to make you plead to the photos. They know you know nothing about it. So that's the situation. That's why I asked you for a definite answer about your plea. Sorry if I sounded like I didn't believe you."

Might as well submit. This man had obviously been appearing in Court since Simon had been at school. Be a bit nicer to him.

"Mmm." said Hopper, staring into space.

"So…you understand then. Just plead not guilty and they will set a trial date. It will probably be in about two months."

Hopper remained distant. "Look I'll see you upstairs," he said as he got up without looking at Simon. He left the cell still carrying his tea.

Simon, armed with no instructions other than the fact that this was a not guilty plea threw his pen onto the table and smiled to himself as he saw it fly off the other side and realised that he would have to go and pick it up. Is that what today is going to be like?

★ ★ ★

Hopper sat alone in his cell. He was pretty nervous about today because it was a long shot but if he pulled it off he would be out of here, free to do as he pleased. He had known about the conspiracy charge since last night. It was no surprise to him. He had effectively engineered it when the Police had interviewed him in prison to see if he knew anything. As if he was going to help them. What could they offer? Dropping the photograph charge? Come on. Anyway, they would never stick to their deal because they never do. Hopper knew this. The Police don't make the decisions, the CPS do. He knew that whatever the Police offered could be over-ruled by some young ambitious prosecutor and he would still be in prison, joined by those he had informed on. All four of them on the same sex offender wing. Help the Police? Not likely.

Hopper's time in prison was spent productively. The idea for what he was going to do came to him while he was listening to the radio. Why had the Police come straight to him? OK, they knew what he was. They knew he could point them in the right direction. But why more or less straight after the abduction? The reason was simple as Hopper knew. They had absolutely no leads. There must have been no descriptions of the men or the car they drove away in. He had spent only a few hours thinking a plan through in his mind. That plan began here today. He had found a way to not only escape a conviction for the conspiracy which, though he actually hadn't been involved in because they were never planned as such , was still a possibility in the current climate where paedophiles were the first enemy of the public, but also to get out of the photographs charge, which he actually was guilty of. It all depended on Simon Silver. He had chosen Simon because he had heard about him from other inmates talking. He knew that he was up and coming. He knew how ambitious lawyers were, how much they want to move from irrelevant and unnoticed cases to big cases that make the papers. He would use that against Simon. Trap him into a corner.

An officer came to the cell door.

"OK Mr Hopper? Time to go up."

Hopper rose to his feet and breathed in slowly. Hopefully this would be the last time he would be contained in a cell. He walked out. The officer accompanied him to the lift and they got inside, arriving shortly afterwards at the holding room behind Court 5. The Court that had extra security measures. Reinforced plastic screens that went up to the roof. A door to the dock that had to be opened with a key. The courtroom for actual criminals, thought Hopper.

Simon was already sitting down as Hopper was brought in. He came straight over to the dock and looked at the dock officer.

"Why is he in handcuffs?" he asked, almost angrily. "No-one said anything to me about that."

The officer looked stunned. He mumbled his words and didn't look Simon in the eye but said something about just doing what the S.O. had told him. Simon sighed. Sometimes, on a practical level, you just have to let go.

"Are you bothered?" he asked his client.

"No it's alright for now," said Hopper calmly, but with a smile to himself that reflected his belief that the risk he was about to take was starting to look like it was going to pay off. Silver was clearly the sort of Barrister that really liked to fight. A good choice.

The Judge was not yet on the Bench. Hopper's case was first on the 10.30 list and HHJ Thompson had gone back to his Chambers to robe up, having sat unrobed for his 10 o'clock list. It was 11.15 now. His Honour seemed to be in no particular hurry.

Caroline Christie walked into Court almost breathless. She was surprised and relieved to see that the Court wasn't sitting. She gave Hopper a quick nod and headed for Simon.

"Sorry! Sorry. God I've been all over this morning. Feels like I've done a day's work already! Anyway, look, can we get a reporting restriction on this case until the trial?"

Simon looked at her and for the second he had remained silent he had tried not to look pleased to see her. He loved this job, but she was the other reason that he got out of bed in the mornings. He fiddled with an elastic band as he looked at her.

"To be honest I could have done with a bit of warning."

Never one to let a woman know how much he wanted her he finished his comment with raised eyebrows. He looked to the floor and sighed, ran a hand through his hair. That should do it.

"OK," he said finally. "Although we can apply to have the trial moved somewhere else if you want."

"Well we just want to make sure that it doesn't make the papers. I don't think moving the trial will make any difference to be honest – this will probably end up on the national news because they haven't found a body yet."

Simon knew that Caroline was right. How stupid of him to say what he had said. Why was it that whenever he was in the presence of a beautiful woman he lost any ability he had to think straight?!

"Alright," he said, "that's a bit pessimistic but fair enough."

Simon regained at least some dignity. Caroline had to think that Simon was a strong individual who didn't need to fall in love but could perhaps be persuaded by the right woman. Apparently women like that, or so he had been told.

"Oh yes, by the way – we still haven't got a full list of exhibits from the CPS about the photos charge."

"Right…"

"So can you tell the Judge? There was an order a month ago for the Pros to serve it within 14 days and we still haven't got it."

"OK will do."

Caroline thanked Simon, put her files on the table behind him and went over to the dock.

"William," she said, "we're going to apply for reporting restrictions ok? We don't want anything to prejudice your trial."

"Thank you," replied Hopper. There's not going to be a trial though. Not with what I've got in mind.

"Hey you don't have to thank me!" she said, trying to create the impression that she was going through the ordeal of the Court hearing with him. He wasn't convinced. He thought she saw an acquittal as a guarantee of more work from Hopper in the future and he was right to think so.

A knock on the Judge's door made everyone stand up, as Simon quickly put his wig on. "Court stand!" bellowed the Usher to an already standing courtroom. The Judge sat down and everyone except Simon followed suit.

"Yes Mr Silver?"

"Your Honour there are a couple of housekeeping matters to attend before the defendant enters a plea."

"Oh?"

"An order was made a month ago by Her Honour Judge Macrae for service of the exhibits in this case within 14 days. This has, unfortunately, not taken place."

"Does it affect the Defendant's plea?"

"I can't really say without sight of them Your Honour."

"Then perhaps he can be arraigned in any event?"

"Indeed Your Honour. However, his plea is based on a case not yet served. Perhaps Your Honour would be minded to urge the Crown to serve the exhibits today?"

The Judge was not happy with this. The Crown had failed to comply with an Order of the Court but since Simon was on his feet he was going to get the brunt of the Judge's frustration.

"I take it, Mr Silver, that those instructing you have taken steps to remind the Crown to serve these exhibits?"

Oh it's like that is it? What do you say to that? It's tempting to lose your temper. But Simon reminded himself that while it is the early bird that catches the worm it is the second mouse that gets the cheese. So slow down.

"Your Honour, I have to say that it is surely outwith the jurisdiction of those instructing me to force the Crown's hand in that way."

Everyone in the room could see that the Judge was less than impressed with that remark.

"Really? Well Mr Silver, I have to say that if you want an adjournment you can have one, but I am minded to make an order for wasted costs on those instructing you. There was no need to come to Court today if you knew you were not ready to enter a plea. You knew the hearing was approaching. You should have done something about it."

Caroline's heart quickened. As did Hopper's. His plan could not tolerate an adjournment.

Simon didn't expect to be threatened with wasted costs. Now he had opened a door. Come on Simon, go for the cheese not the worm.

"Your Honour," said Simon, slowly – not so much for effect as for stalling for a few more seconds in order to think of something to say. Come on, they're all watching. Come on! Silence. Got it!

"Those instructing me did originally send letters to the CPS to request the exhibits. They did not, however, delay in serving a defence statement as they could be excused for having done." Pause. For effect this time. "Instead, they abandoned this campaign of polite persuasion, opting for an application for an order of the Court. That order was made. To ask those instructing to continue to make their requests in the light of such an order would surely be to suggest that further Solicitors' letters would carry more weight than an order from a Learned Judge? That surely cannot be right. Is this the day when all Judges in the jurisdiction are effectively made redundant?"

Stunned silence. Where the hell had that come from? He wondered whether he had appeared convincing or just plain laughable.

"Yes I take the point Mr Silver. Exhibits today please Mr Riley."

"Yes Your Honour," replied Riley standing up and sitting down in one movement.

"I hadn't thought of it like that Mr Silver. Interesting."

You'll do for me, thought Hopper, beginning to get quite excited. Caroline was pretty impressed too.

"You said there were a couple of things Mr Silver," remarked the Judge.

Did I? Shit. Being madly in love with Caroline did have its advantages sometimes. This was one of those times. She was always in his mind somewhere and as he searched for something to say she came unwittingly to his rescue.

"Your Honour, I also make an application for a certificate for litigation support at the trial."

You're supposed to do that after a not guilty plea but it'll do.

"Oh yes – this is certainly a case that merits support from instructing Solicitors. Can the Defendant be arraigned now?"

"Yes Your Honour, though I daresay it will come as no surprise to the Court what that plea will be given the application I have just made! I apologise for having taken so much time." You have to give them something.

The Court Clerk rose.

"Stand up please," she said.

Hopper stood up.

"Are you William Hopper?"

"I am."

"William Hopper you are charged on this indictment containing two Counts. On Count 1 you are charged with taking indecent photographs of children. The particulars of the offence are that you on a date between 12th August 2001 and 17th August 2001 took indecent photographs of a child as she undressed in her home. Are you guilty or not guilty?"

"Not guilty."

"Not guilty," repeated the Clerk as she wrote the plea on her copy of the indictment.

"On Count 2 you are charged with Conspiracy to Abduct. The particulars of the offence are that you, on a date between 12th August 2001 and 14th December 2001 conspired with others unknown to abduct a child. Are you guilty or not guilty?"

Hopper's heart was racing now. This was it. The moment when he implemented the first part of his plan. The moment from which there would be no going back.

"Not guilty." He was almost shaking now.

"Not guilty," repeated the Clerk, endorsing the Court's copy of the indictment.

"But I know where she is."

Now it has started. No going back now.

Hopper only saw the Judge but everyone's eyes were on him. A woman in the public gallery began to cry noticeably.

"Mr Hopper, what did you say?" asked the Judge.

Now the test. Can you stay silent at a time like this?

"Mr Hopper?"

Hopper stood bolt upright, holding the Judge's gaze. And

he remained totally silent, concentrating only on his breathing, *You're doing well.*

"MR HOPPER?!"

The members of the press gallery were all writing furiously now, which reminded Simon of the second thing he was supposed to have applied for.

Still Hopper's silence persisted.

Simon rose to his feet.

"Your Honour, the defendant's remark has come of something of a surprise to everyone, not least to me. I wonder if it might be prudent to allow me a few minutes to speak to Mr Hopper in the room behind the dock?"

The Judge leant forward and pointed at Simon.

"I want to know why your client is refusing to answer my question Mr Silver."

"Your Honour, I find myself wholly disarmed and can only offer my own personal apology in advance of that which will I'm sure follow from the defendant once I have had the chance to speak to him."

"Two minutes Mr Silver."

The dock officer opened the door to the dock to allow Simon and Caroline through. The door to the Court then closed behind them and only Simon remained standing.

"Right – you are going to have to explain yourself in there. And apologise. That kid's poor mother is sitting in the dock in floods of tears. You are doing yourself no favours."

Silence.

Caroline, sitting next to Hopper in an effort to look supportive of him said, "William, come on, you don't want to wind this Judge up – he might end up being the one who sits in the trial."

He remained silent.

"Hey come on, don't do this ok?" said Simon.

"I want a reporting restriction. Then I'll talk."

"Whoa, this is absolutely not the time to be making demands. Seriously."

Hopper stayed silent as he looked slowly up at Simon with raised eyebrows as if to say that this absolutely was the time to be making demands actually.

"I've said all I am going to say at this juncture. You have your instructions."

Simon wondered why he had got out of bed this morning. He should have been sitting in the Advocate's lounge talking about yesterday's trial by now. He looked at Caroline and sighed.

"Right, well if that's the way you want to play it, then…" he shrugged his shoulders. What the hell was he going to tell the Judge now?

They all went back into Court 5. His Honour Judge Thompson looked at Mr Silver, earnestly awaiting the apology that he had been promised.

"Your Honour I find myself in a very precarious situation. The Defendant will not speak even to me unless he gets a reporting restriction."

The Judge's face reddened.

"I will not be dictated to by that man!" he shouted. "There will be no reporting restriction. And Hopper will answer my question."

Hopper then looked towards the public gallery. Julie was still crying. Maybe she was his ticket out of here. This was unexpected. He didn't think the family would be here but the Police must have told them. He looked at the Judge, folded his arms and pointed to Julie by nodding his head in her direction once his eyes had met those of the Judge.

The Judge, now furious, looked at Simon.

"Mr Silver, I take it you have explained to the defendant

the consequences of his behaviour?"

As Simon stood up, so did Hopper.

"Sit down Hopper. SIT DOWN! I gave you the opportunity to explain yourself and you didn't take it."

"Your Honour," said Hopper in a calm voice, "that girl is still alive. And I know where she is. But if you allow the press to report this, particularly on the television then the people who have her will be alerted to the fact that they are in danger of being found. And they will leave where they are. They won't want to take their new friend with them will they? What will happen to her, the little girl who can give the Police a description of them? I dread to think. Give me what I want and then I'll talk more. Oh, and Your Honour – you WILL be dictated to by me. Don't sign a death warrant just because you feel territorial about the Court you command. I'm not impressed by you. You wouldn't want blood on your hands would you? And you wouldn't want that either would you Mrs Taylor?" he said, his eyes still fixed as they had been on the Judge.

Julie was uncontrollable now – her tears turned into fierce anger as Paul tried in vain to hold her back. She ran out of the public gallery and towards the dock. She hammered on the plastic that separated her from Hopper.

"WHERE IS MY DAUGHTER?! YOU SICK EVIL BASTARD! WHERE IS SHE?! I WANT MY DAUGHTER!"

Hopper remained perfectly calm as he watched Julie shout until she collapsed crying. He smiled down at her. The Usher helped Julie to her feet and looked up at the Judge for instructions.

"Mrs Taylor," said the Judge in a calm voice, "the Court cannot tolerate that. Please sit down. Please. Could you get her some water?" The Usher nodded and the Judge went on. "Mrs Taylor, please let me deal with this. I'm so sorry – I have children, grandchildren. This must be the most unimaginable ordeal. But please let me deal with it – you really must remain seated if you want to remain in Court."

He turned back to Hopper.

"Where is she?" asked the Judge, this time in a calm voice as he thought of his own grandchildren.

Silence.

"I don't think he knows at all," said the Judge, knowing that to assume so would be to take the greatest of risks.

"Oh I do," said Hopper," I just haven't heard what I need to hear yet."

The Judge sat for a moment. Why had this Conspiracy Count been added? There must be some reason for it. Maybe he did know where she was. Wasting time now might prove fatal.

"Very well," he said, "no reporting on this matter until further notice." He could not believe what he was doing. "Now you tell me where she is."

The faces on the members of the press assembled in Court fell and the collective sighs were audible above the silence. The Judge chose to ignore them.

"Oh there's more to come yet," said Hopper as he rose up out of his seat and walked through the door to the holding area that the dock officer, he noticed, had not locked.

What does a Judge do in this situation? He was getting out of even his depth now. This was such an unprecedented turn of events that he was having to adlib the whole thing. He was doing a fine job in truth. He had been understanding with Julie's outburst, he had not made a fuss when the press members had sighed rudely. He wasn't even blaming Simon. But he was running out of ideas now.

"I shall rise now," said the Judge. "Mr Silver, perhaps you could ask my Clerk to contact me when you have seen the defendant. I expect that's where you are going."

"I shall Your Honour."

"In fact come to my Chambers once you are finished with him. Um...don't take too long Mr Silver."

"Your Honour, yes."

FIFTEEN

Simon looked round at Caroline. The whole room was gobsmacked. Some people had had notice of the fact that Hopper might know something about Hannah's kidnap – to others, including Simon, this was totally new. It seemed as though the Judge had given up, letting Simon deal with the problem. The public gallery was silent, as though they were waiting for someone in a wig to say something. As it was, the Court Usher broke the silence and told the public that they might as well leave Court, perhaps get a cup of coffee and some fresh air. He promised them that he would put a call out for them over the public address when the Court was ready to reconvene but warned them that this may be a matter of hours rather than minutes since no Court sat between one and two o'clock.

Alan Riley looked at Simon.

"Well, it looks like you're in for a busy day!" He gathered up some papers and turned to walk out of Court.

"I'll wait to hear from you downstairs."

Alan Riley would now go and sit in the Advocates' Lounge. He would be telling the story to everyone. Simon wished he could be there too but he knew he had to go to see Hopper in the cells. The story would be old news by the time Simon was in a position to tell it. He stopped himself. He had a vision of a little girl he had never met. What if Hopper really did know where she was? She was definitely missing – was she still alive? What was she doing right now? More importantly what were the people who took her doing right now? Simon felt guilty for thinking about sitting downstairs and telling stories. Suddenly he felt the need to act and quickly – if Hopper could help the Police find the girl, Simon was wasting time standing around thinking about it.

He turned to Caroline who was still sitting down behind him. She looked up at him.

"I suppose we'd better go downstairs," he said.

She gathered up her files.

"I'll need you there Caroline – I need a full note of what we discuss. Everything. I don't like this guy. He's obviously a nutcase. I don't want to end up in a his-word-against-mine situation when he gets his life sentence!"

"No, definitely – I'll make sure we're all backed up"

They left the Court and, passing the public gallery, noticed the girl's family.

Simon didn't know who was who, apart from Mrs Taylor. She was in the company of four large men, one of whom Simon assumed would be the girl's father. All five of them looked up at Simon. Nothing was said. Nothing needed to be said. They looked at him intently but without obvious menace, though their eyes hinted at hatred. And yet they seemed earnest too – as though asking that which they despised for help. He could bring her back. He was defending a monster, but he might help them. A curious balance of emotions on their part. A curious inability to assess the meaning of their stares on Simon's.

Simon had not held their gaze. He had only looked at them briefly while he walked to the door. What did his eyes convey to them? He looked almost apologetic. Maybe he didn't enjoy what he was doing. Perhaps he was sorry for the heartache that his client was causing. Maybe he looked hopeful, like he wanted to find out where Hannah was too. Simon and Caroline left the

Court and took the lift down to the cells.

Hopper was already causing a stir in the cells. He had not been violent – if anything he had been polite and almost gentlemanly. He had walked to the door of a cell and waited silently to be let in. He knew he wouldn't need to be inside the cell for very long – Silver was probably racing down the stairs to have a word with this now famous client. What a parasite he was. Riding on the back of Hopper's great plan, to emerge the valiant lawyer, guiding the Court to the location of a kidnapped girl. All of the staff were talking about what he had said in Court. They had heard about Hannah Taylor on the news. They had seen the appeals, they had seen her parents' images on the television. They had all seen a photograph of Hannah on the television and in the papers. They were almost as excited as Hopper was that Silver was coming down to the cells. They were all dying to see what would happen next.

A buzzer sounded in the cell area and was answered enthusiastically.

"Court Cells".

"Counsel to see Mr Hopper".

The door was opened and Simon was allowed in. Caroline followed.

They both sat down in a conference room with three chairs and a table. A room empty other than that, which would have symbolised Simon's mind given his having drawn a blank as to what on earth to do next, were it not for the fact that all of the conference cells were equally grey and empty.

Hopper was sent for and soon came walking up the corridor. He walked into the room and looked at Simon. His face made him look proud, as though he was the grand engineer of his Barrister's predicament. He was of course. But it seemed to please him more than it should. His face changed when he saw Caroline.

"Have a seat Mr Hopper," said Simon, pointing to the unoccupied chair.

Hopper remained standing.

"She goes," he said, all the while looking at Simon.

"No, Mr Hopper, she stays. She leaves when I do. Sit down please."

Hopper recognised the challenge he now faced.

"There are other Barristers Mr Silver," he said patronisingly.

"Then instruct one," said Simon, standing up.

Hopper smiled and let out the tiniest of laughs.

"But that would mean an adjournment, Mr Silver. Little girly can't wait you know."

"No it wouldn't. Someone could take this case right now, like I did this morning."

A fair point. Shit. Although…

"Maybe. But don't you want the case? Don't you want to be the hero? You can be the one who saves her. I'll make you famous."

"Mr Hopper, I want her here to take notes."

Damn. Shouldn't have said that.

Hopper turned to leave the conference cell.

"I wonder what they are doing to her right now," he said to himself as he opened the door.

Simon looked to Caroline. Maybe she should make this decision.

"It's ok I'll leave," she said.

"You have a chat," said Hopper, realising that he had obviously made some sense to Caroline if not to Silver, "I'm going back to my cell." He left, closing the door behind him.

Simon spoke next.

"I need you here. I need someone here with me."

"But if he instructs someone else it will mean wasting time.

I really think he knows where she is."

"He can't instruct anyone else. There's no reason to. Anyway, the Judge won't have it. He will see the same wasted time that you do."

"Then you are stuck with him on your own. I have to go – if I stay here then I am the reason that girl isn't found. I can't be that reason. This is my role in helping her."

"I'm not convinced he does know anything," said Simon though he thought he probably did.

"Why do you think they've stuck this extra charge on? The Police think he knows. He's playing into their hands. They'll get what they want and then continue to prosecute him for the photos – you know what they're like."

Simon thought that made sense. He would be tempted by an offer that he would jump at. The girl would be found and they would just keep going on the photos. It happened that way sometimes. People make deals to save their friend or girlfriend from staying in the case and then get hammered on sentence. There's no way they would let him go. But then Simon had seen the way that Hopper appeared to know his way around the Court system. He wouldn't be fooled by this. He wouldn't risk being kept in prison with whoever he told them had taken Hannah. They would know it was him. God knows what they would do to him. Anyway, they wouldn't release him until they found the girl alive. Simon thought further. Their priority was not to arrest anyone – it was to save Hannah. Doing both would be ideal and by finding her they might find the men who took her. But then Hopper would know this and wouldn't want to risk it. They would kill him in prison. What was he doing? Maybe he was going to give them false information. But then that wouldn't help him – there was no way they would let him go until they found her.

But what if she had been killed by now? Hopper would

gain nothing from this. Simon wasn't constricted by time – he was being helped by it! Every minute that passed should make Hopper more and more anxious. He would end up telling them everything. Simon didn't really need Caroline there after all. Time would replace her as his assistant. He would just sit with Hopper and watch him concede. He wouldn't look so cocky then. Truth be told, Hopper wasn't anxious in the slightest and Simon would soon find out why.

Caroline left the cell and Simon waited for her to be ushered through the security doors. Once she had gone through, he asked for Hopper to brought round again. He arrived within a minute. Simon was already sitting back down when Hopper came back in and, noticing Caroline having left, he smiled.

"Ah, Mr Silver, my faith in humanity is renewed".

He sat down and waited for Simon to speak. Simon seemed to be waiting for Hopper to speak but since he obviously wasn't going to, Simon thought it best to begin.

"So what the hell was that all about upstairs?"

"Just telling it like it is Mr Silver".

"So you really do know where she is?"

"Of course I do." And he seemed to mean it.

"Well, where?"

"Oh come on Mr Silver, I need to see your cards first. I'm not going to sit in a cell while they wander off to find her. I'm not stupid. I need my reward you know."

"What do you mean my cards?"

"I want certain guarantees."

"I can't guarantee anything – I don't make that sort of decision."

"But you get to speak to the man who does. And in his Chambers so you don't have to worry about looking useless in public."

Simon paused. He wasn't going to rise to this.

"So what do you want?"

"I want all the charges to disappear. I want to be released. I want to be moved out of the area and given a new name. And in return I offer the...locus in quo, the place where you will find girly."

Simon laughed in disbelief.

"That's quite a shopping list Mr Hopper. And you know there's no way they'll let you go before they have found her. They won't trust you like that."

"Of course not. That's why the information will be given in stages."

"How do you mean?"

"Each time I get something I want, I will take them closer to where she is. So far I have been given a reporting restriction. In exchange I will tell you that when they took the girly they headed north on the A1. Now you can go and tell the Judge that."

"If I go in there with that I will look ridiculous. Tell me everything and I will argue for you in stages, in the way that you instruct me."

"But Mr Silver, that would be to suggest that I trust you. Please don't be fooled into thinking that."

"Then what the fuck am I doing here?!"

Simon was getting wound up now. They tell you not to let clients get to you, but this one was. Hopper leant forward, as though welcoming Simon's raised voice rather than fearing it.

"Because you are young, Simon. Ambitious. Malleable."

He had not called him Simon before now. It was as though this slight change in address made a huge difference. He seemed different now. Or maybe what was different was that Simon had realised that he was briefed to cover this case personally not for his skills but for his lack of skills.

"Simon, let me ask you something. What do you say to people when they ask you how you defend people when you know they are guilty? People must ask you that question quite often don't they? Uninitiated friends. Family members proud of you yet slightly wary at the same time."

Simon always gave the same answer to that but wondered why he was even entertaining the question. He answered anyway, perhaps curious as to where it was going.

"I tell them that you never know whether someone is guilty or not, that you weren't there when the alleged event happened. I tell them that it is for the Jury to decide whether someone is guilty or not."

"But they don't believe you I bet. They say to you 'come on Simon, you must be able to tell'"

"Sometimes they do."

"But what if the client tells you they are guilty Simon, what do you do then?"

Please do it Hopper. Please. Then I can withdraw.

"Then I either tell them to plead guilty or I withdraw from the case and tell them to instruct someone else."

"But what if they *won't* plead guilty?"

"Then I withdraw."

"And what if you don't? Come on, Simon, who would know?"

Simon started to see where this was going now.

"If I am ever found out then I would be in hot water. I would probably lose my position."

"That's entirely correct, Simon, top marks."

Hopper's voice lessened.

"Now Simon I want you to listen very carefully. You are going to get me out of here. You are going to make sure that I get a new name and get to live out of the north east. If you don't do exactly what I tell you to do then I will not offer the information and they can dig girly up when I finish my sentence. I will stand trial for the photos and the conspiracy and I will inform the Bar Council and your inn, which I believe is the Inner Temple?" he smiled, "that you continued to represent me despite the fact that I had told you I was guilty."

"Fuck you!" shouted Simon, getting up, "you are living in a fantasy world. You can't trap me like that."

"Simon, Simon, you should have had the good sense to have your Solicitor here taking a full note of what was said. Now you are all on your own."

Hopper sat back and folded his arms.

Simon now realised why Hopper had not been worried. He had planned it like this all along. Preyed on Simon's sense of humanity, knowing that he would want to help the girl. He was still standing.

"Come back down when you've spoken to the Judge," said Hopper. And he knew that Simon would be speaking to the Judge.

★ ★ ★

Simon left the cells and sighed angrily. He hated today already – it was already the worst day of his career. Worse than writing Donald Ramsey's advices and not getting paid for it. Simon knew that he was no genius, he just had a unique mind. All his life he had been quick to accept his fate. He had rarely sulked – he tended to just get on with things, making the best of bad situations. It was this characteristic that had so far served him well as a Barrister. And by the time he had walked the short distance to the lifts he had accepted his own conclusion that he was in a position of unusual importance. Hannah Taylor had been kidnapped and could perhaps be found. This he knew. His conclusion was that in order for this to happen, he would have to do everything that he could to get Hopper out of the Court building. And that meant doing exactly what he asked.

As Simon approached Court 5, Hannah's family was outside. They weren't waiting to lynch him but he felt as though they were. One of the men got up and walked over to Simon. Simon tensed up, worried that the man, who was considerably larger than him, was going to hit him. He should keep walking. He stopped. The man's pace slowed. This was no attack. The man looked weary, as though it had been a challenge to walk over to Simon. And he looked nervous too. He was talking to a Barrister, which shouldn't be impressive, but did command a sense of respect. His voice was soft.

"Has he said where Hannah is yet?"

Simon wanted to tell him. But to be seen talking to the family would not look good. He was, after all, in character. The whole building was covered by cameras, someone might see and so while there was no-one in the immediate vicinity, Simon pushed on. He turned to the man, all the while walking backwards.

"I'm sorry," he said, "really, I actually am, but I really can't talk to you. Liaise with Mr Riley. I will tell him everything that I know." Riley. Shit, he's downstairs. He will have to come into Chambers too. Simon turned about and went back towards the family. As he walked past he heard a voice say "he's probably one himself". He knew what that meant. But he said nothing.

Alan Riley was reading the paper when Simon walked into the lounge.

"Alan!" he shouted to him.

Alan looked over the top of *The Times*.

Simon didn't want to engage in conversation and so opted instead for a hand gesture to indicate going upstairs. Alan knew what this meant and got out of his chair. Simon took advantage of his head start and went straight back to the lifts and made sure he didn't hold the door open while Alan put on his robe and wig. He walked along past the family again. He felt them looking at him, but didn't look back. Alan could deal with them.

He arrived soon after Simon. All five members of the family stood up expectantly. Alan anticipated their question and raised his palms.

"Nothing yet I'm afraid," he said, though he didn't appear particularly apologetic, "I'll update you as we go," he added as he walked into Court.

Simon was already there of course. The Clerk of the Court had telephoned through to the Judge and looked at Alan as he came through the door.

"Mr Riley, the Judge is ready for you both." The Usher took them both through to the Judge's Chambers.

"Have a seat," said Charles Thompson. He was sitting down behind his desk in the middle of what was probably his tenth cup of coffee since the farce that had been the PDH half an hour ago. He looked at Simon. As did Alan.

"What's the situation?" asked Charles.

Simon cleared his throat and looked at Charles in a man-to-man fashion.

"Can I just say first that I am totally bewildered by this. I playing this totally by ear and I just want you both to know I'm not trying to hide anything. It's all a bit unfamiliar to be honest."

"It's alright Simon. I think we all feel pretty much the same." He looked at Alan, who agreed with a raise of his eyebrows.

"Well, thanks, er...right, basically Hopper is still making demands. He does appear to know where the girl, Hannah, is and he wants me to thank you for the reporting restriction by telling you that after the kidnap the men took the A1 northbound. That's all he will tell me at the moment."

"Well that's not much use is it?" said Charles.

"It's not, no. But," he sighed, "he says you will find out more later. He wants to do it in stages. Which reflects the fact that he wants certain guarantees."

Neither man looked surprised. Maybe they had seen this situation before. If that was the case, how was Simon doing?

"I thought it might go this way. Are you sure he knows where she is?"

"Here I am almost sticking up for him! Judge, I told him that there was no way that you would release him until the Police found the girl. Hannah."

"Release him?! You have got to be kidding! He has as good as admitted his part in the conspiracy! I can't just let him go!"

Simon was puzzled.

"I thought the count was added just today – to ensure a plea to the photos."

Alan looked at Simon, the man twenty years his junior with a look of pity.

"Come on Simon – that's a bit far-fetched!"

Simon thought back to what Alan had told him earlier. He had totally misled him and was now acting as though the conversation had never taken place.

Alan looked slightly on edge as Simon looked back at him with eyes that showed helpless disgust. Instead, to Alan's relief, of Simon saying anything about it he looked to Charles.

"Maybe I am paranoid by nature. Or naïve. What did you mean he has admitted to his part?"

"Well that's why the Count was added. He as much as told the Police, on tape, that he had helped organise the kidnap while he was in prison, by letter and phone calls. How don't you know about this Simon?"

Either drop Alan in it, which he deserves. Or say you haven't fully read the brief and look unprofessional. Riley had

25 years' call. Simon didn't.

"I mustn't have all the facts then. There's nothing in my brief about that."

Even better, now it's someone else's fault. Ideal.

"Well," continued Charles, "last night, the night of the kidnap, he apparently told a prison officer he had information as to the girl's whereabouts. The Officer called the Police and they came straight over to the prison to interview him."

Alan cut in, "we had the count added this morning. OK maybe that's a bit unorthodox but in the light of a confession it's a bit like a TiC."

"No it isn't," replied Simon, "but I can see what you mean." He sighed. "None of that matters now anyway – if you've got an admission then the Count will stay or he will be tried for it separately in a few months' time. We can't risk finding the girl murdered when we might find her alive."

It was unorthodox. But Simon found himself agreeing with Riley's course of action, especially given what was at stake. He would have preferred some notice though. And to be allowed to hear the tape with this so-called confession. There was a silence and Charles spoke next.

"You're right Simon, nothing at all would be given to Hopper unless and until the girl is found alive. And so he has nothing to gain by lying about it. In fact, if he was lying and asking for charges to be dropped he would then face another charge or attempting to pervert the course of justice."

"Then he must definitely know. That carries a sentence higher than the photographs do. It would make no sense for him to lie," said Simon both to himself and to the group.

"It would appear so," agreed Charles.

"So what does he want?" asked Alan.

"He wants all charges to be discontinued, to be released, given a new name and be moved out of the area."

They didn't scoff. Which was surprising since it was a lot to ask. But then it was more than a fair exchange for a little girl's life. Of course it was. But then perhaps not in terms of the future.

Charles looked at Alan and then at Simon.

"I want the names of the other conspirators Simon."

Simon had not thought about that. It wouldn't matter though; once the Police found the girl they would find the men anyway. That was obviously why Hopper wanted to be given a new identity.

"I should go back and talk to Hopper. What can I tell him?"

"Nothing yet," replied Charles, "I need more than northbound on the A1 before thinking about staying the indictment."

"Then I will tell him just that."

Simon got up, as did Alan, who followed him out of Chambers.

"Simon," said Alan, "thanks".

Alan looked different now.

"You could have dropped me right in it there. Thanks for, you know, not doing it."

"You being unprofessional doesn't matter to me Alan, I just know not to trust you in the future." He kept walking.

"Alright. Simon, Simon!" said Alan, catching up, "look – my hands are as tied as I imagine yours are. I will help as much as I can with the Police ok? You can at least believe me when I say I want that girl found."

"She's called Hannah," said Simon and walked away. It was a bit trite, but it felt dramatic.

Simon walked back into the cells. He didn't even need to ask to see Hopper – he was walking up the corridor as Simon was walking down it. They both entered a conference cell and sat down.

"So?" asked Hopper.

"I think we're getting some way to getting the indictment stayed. But the Judge wants more than what you said about the A1".

Hopper sat silently for a moment. He looked annoyed. But then he smiled.

"Procedures eh?" he said.

Simon did not return the chuckle that then followed.

"Very well Simon," Hopper continued, "this is what we'll do. We go back into Court and I get formal not guilty verdicts on both Counts and then I will tell the Court more."

Simon said nothing. He got up and walked back upstairs. He could see he was going to have to find Alan like before and then wait for him. Like before. This was already getting tedious. Instead, he called down to reception over the internal telephone and asked them to call Alan Riley to Court 5. He would just meet him there.

Charles Thompson was not impressed.

"That's too much for what might still be nothing Simon. Once I've said that in open Court I can only keep him in for contempt if he then decides to say nothing. This looks like a rouse to get out of a sticky situation. Because otherwise he would be free to go and we would be no further forward."

Alan spoke next.

"Judge, why don't we just discontinue the photos? Then we can see what he tells us. If he says nothing then we still have the conspiracy and we can add attempt to pervert like you said earlier. And if you reserve the case to yourself you can add a bit more onto the sentence for the photos, without actually saying so."

Charles and Simon both looked surprised. Simon at Alan's audacity. Charles at the very good idea.

"I'm happy to do that. Thank you Alan. Simon?"

That bastard. It was almost worth fighting Hopper's corner just to show Riley up. Prick. But come on, what about Hannah? Riley could wait – she couldn't.

"Sounds fair enough I suppose. Shall we do it now?"

"Don't you want to see Hopper first?" asked Charles.

"I can tell him this in the dock. I have a feeling he might get a shock and then start talking."

★ ★ ★

Hopper was brought up as all parties were called to Court 5. Simon told Caroline what was happening as she came in and sat down behind him. She could do no more than assure Simon that she at least got a full note of what was said in Court.

Simon approached the dock. Caroline felt the need not to follow.

"Mr Hopper, they are going to drop the photos, but the conspiracy will have to stay."

"Thought so," he replied looking excited, "it's strange you know, I'm actually only guilty of taking the photos!" he smiled.

Simon wondered what he meant. Had he not confessed to the conspiracy? Why? That would carry a higher sentence than the photos. The Usher knocked on the door and Simon hurried back to his seat as HHJ Thompson walked in. Shit. Forgot to tell Hopper something.

"Your Honour, forgive me, I hadn't quite finished telling the Defendant the…situation."

"Quite alright Mr Silver, feel free."

Simon returned to the dock.

"Hey look – you better not be bullshitting. If you don't give them any more information then they will get you on perverting the course of justice. And they *will* get you I guarantee that much."

"Sneaky," said Hopper almost cheekily, "fair enough Simon, I understand". He sat down. Simon walked back to his seat. Stop calling me Simon you fucking weasel.

Alan stood up.

"Yes Mr Riley."

"Your Honour, after very careful consideration of the Crown's case against the Defendant in relation to Count one of the indictment, it has been decided that no evidence will be offered upon that Count, that is to say the taking of indecent photographs of children."

Alan sat down.

"Observations Mr Silver?"

"Your Honour I would ask that a formal verdict of Not Guilty be returned on Count one of this indictment."

"Very well, I return a formal verdict of Not Guilty to Count 1. Now Mr Hopper I believe you have something you want to tell me."

Hannah's family sat behind the dark screen that separated the public gallery from the main body of the Court. They could see Hopper but he could not see them. He knew they were there of course. They were all looking directly at him, waiting for him to speak. They had been told that he had admitted to having been involved in the conspiracy and while he was obviously part of the reason why she was taken he was also about to become the reason why they got her back. For their part they believed Hopper, perhaps because they needed to believe him. This was a normal reaction, one which Hopper had predicted.

Hopper looked blankly at the Judge. They were all waiting for him to speak. The family were praying for him to speak. And so he took a moment and enjoyed the silence. He preferred the silence. He felt alive within it, especially in silence such as this which he could command. It would stay silent for as long as he wished. No-one could override him while he was in control. Eventually he tired of it. He was enjoying the moment but felt the need to speed things up, to chase the eventual thrill that his love of silence would not itself override. The thrill of being the one who led the Police to Hannah. The thrill of being released. The thrill of being back out there.

"When they took her, they headed north on the A1."

"Yes, Mr Hopper, we know that," said Charles.

At least that showed that they believed him. They *knew*. That's what the Judge had just said. He could have said 'you told us that earlier' or 'so you say' but he had said that they *knew*. This really was working.

"But her family don't know that Your Honour. You really ought to think about them you know. Imagine what they are going through while you sit there in your big chair. Their daughter's life is in your hands."

Charles Thompson was getting angry. He was about to add a charge of perverting the course of justice right there and then but something told him to wait. A lack of evidence perhaps.

"They drove away in a black people-carrier. That's right isn't it Mr Taylor?"

Paul's heart quickened. He really did know. Hopper had said the people-carrier was black. Paul seemed to remember it being black now.

"They travelled north for…an hour or so without stopping."

Only Hannah and the three men knew that that was not quite true.

"They crossed the border into Scotland and headed east along minor roads. Through the Lammermuir Hills, through the Moorfoot Hills." He paused. "And that's all you will get from me for now. I will be waiting for the second formal verdict." He turned to leave but the dock officer had locked the door this time.

Charles looked towards Alan.

"Perhaps you need to consider your position Mr Riley," he said, "I will rise now to give you an opportunity to do so".

Charles had the answer he needed. He looked to the family sat in the public gallery for acknowledgement but received none. They needed more.

"Don't waste any time Mr Riley," he said and left the Court.

It was obvious now that Hopper did know where Hannah was. The media had made no mention of a black people-carrier. Hopper could not have guessed this surely? And then to describe a journey in detail...There was no way he could be so specific. He must have been involved. It came as a strange sense of relief to the family that they now had, at least, confirmation that Hannah would be found. But to them this was still only confirmation that she would be found and did not necessarily mean that she would be saved. Simon knew this too. And while he had told them that he could not speak to them, the fact that Alan Riley had rushed past them to go downstairs to the CPS room to discuss matters with the Police made him feel that it was his moral duty to say at least something to ease their pain as far as he could. He knew he shouldn't, but this was not an ordinary day in Court and he felt justified in bending the rules. He walked over.

He looked at the family uneasily. They looked at him with more hate than they had before. He was the reason they were still waiting. Why was he defending Hopper now? He knew he was involved. How could he do it? Try to represent the legal interests of someone like this? But Simon didn't create the law, it existed before his career began. And he nestled comfortably into this excuse and immersed himself in its softness every time a situation tested his moral reserve. They wouldn't know how much it was doing to Simon. They wouldn't care and perhaps rightly so. But in truth, what other way was there?

"I dare say you heard all that," he said to them. Of course they had. They had probably been listening more intently than he had himself.

"I've spoken to him and to be honest there's no point in his making anything up. He said earlier that Hannah is still alive and I believe him. I want you to know that he won't walk out of here today without Hannah being found alive. So please, bear that in mind. He can even be charged with a separate offence if it turns out he was lying."

He left them with this good news, which it was as far as he was concerned. If it was true. If she still was alive. Simon had a feeling that he had just made a promise that might not be delivered.

The Officers in the case had been in Court but they had reconvened in the CPS room for no real reason other than for the fact that it was familiar territory for them. Lowry sent PC David Whelan to find a road atlas while he and Alan Riley discussed the next move, with Austin very much in the background.

"Looks rather like he does know where she is," Alan remarked.

"So why won't he say more?"

"He wants to chuck the conspiracy charge."

Lowry laughed.

"With all due respect Mr Riley you can fuck right off if you think I'm having that. No chance. That would mean him walking out of here a free man. There's no way you're dropping it – he admitted to it."

"I know. But he won't say any more until it goes."

"But if it goes then so does he! Once there's a formal not guilty he can just leave the dock. He doesn't need to say anything at all! It's obvious what he's doing. He's just leaving little clues which are probably just coincidences. Anyone could have made up what he just said up there."

"But he knew about the people-carrier."

Lowry sighed and covered his face with his hands.

"No-one can contradict him. It's not like we know the car to have been dark blue."

Alan looked at Lowry and felt pity for his two-dimensional logic.

"There is something else though. He knows that if he is lying he will not be released and will face another indictment."

"Well I'm not having him back on the street to do this to other children."

That is all very forward-looking. It seemed to Alan that Lowry had as good as given up. "What about Hannah?" he asked, using her name for the first time.

Lowry sighed. "I don't know how to balance this. In a way something tells me that to lose her and save…I don't know how many others…is worth doing."

Perhaps some of Simon's compassion had rubbed off on Alan Riley. Maybe old dogs can learn new tricks.

"Just you think about what you are saying Lowry. If I was twenty years younger you'd be lying on the floor right now." And he meant it.

Lowry didn't fear Riley. He was too old to be taken seriously as far as threats of violence were concerned. But he was right. And Lowry felt belittled. He exhaled deeply.

"I don't know why I said that. I'm just really concerned at what he might do if he gets out. Fucking hell Alan, he's a monster, you know?"

"I know. And that's why you will no doubt keep a constant

eye on him if he gets out. You get to be the person who makes sure he never harms a child."

PC Whelan arrived in the CPS room carrying a road atlas. It was lucky that he had one in his car. There wasn't one in the CPS room.

"Right David," said Lowry, "let's see about this route. A1 northbound across the border." He moved his finger along the road. "That would mean they crossed the border just by Berwick. They must have gone east fairly soon after though, cos look – otherwise they would end up in Edinburgh which is further north than the Lammermuir Hills."

He paused.

"There aren't many minor roads that I can see on here mind you, ones that go through the Lammermuir area."

"Sir, look – this would make sense," said Whelan who added his finger to the map and drew it across a smaller road. "They would have gone along here – it takes you through the Moorfoot Hills as well."

"But where after that?" asked Lowry, "look – it takes you back into England that way." He looked at Alan. "Maybe he is just making this up Alan. He knows the main road from London to Edinburgh. And he knows the name of a couple of hill ranges. It's not enough."

Austin walked over and looked closely at the map.

"He's stopped talking at the right place hasn't he? There are a thousand routes you could take after the Moorfoot Hills."

"So they could have gone anywhere in Scotland, or even back to England," Lowry said in a lowered voice. "So we know absolutely fuck all?" his voice noticeably louder this time as he walked over to the window, one hand one his hip and the other brushing his hair back.

Alan looked at Whelan and Austin.

"We'll just have to wait to hear from Silver."

This time Hopper was waiting for Simon in a conference cell.

"Have a seat, Simon," he said as though it was his room and he was entertaining a guest. Simon at down and placed his papers on the desk. It was starting to be the case that nothing surprised Simon now. Hopper had crossed the line into a place where he could generate no offence. Simon just wanted to go home. For this to be over. He looked at Hopper.

"What did you mean earlier – you said you weren't guilty of the conspiracy?"

Hopper smiled at him, as though he was about to ease Simon gently into the workings of his mind, looking down on him with almost pity that he just didn't understand.

"Exactly that. I had nothing to do with it."

"But you confessed to it! You invited the Police to the prison. It's on tape!"

Hopper shook his head.

"And so are telephone calls from prison phones. They are probably being analysed right now."

"I don't understand."

"I know you don't Simon. You only see conference rooms when you go into prisons don't you?" He seemed sympathetic. He continued. "Don't you think they read all of my letters coming in and letters I send out? Of course they do. There is even an official position for the people who read it. I always get my mail opened. They don't hide it. They don't have to. No-one believes criminals anyway. And when you get released you are so glad to be out you don't bother making a fuss about it. Look Simon, I couldn't really do very much conspiring from prison – they read letters and listen to phone calls."

"Then why say you were involved in the kidnap? You'll be convicted on your confession alone! It's not like they beat it out of you – you invited them over!"

"I'll never stand trial for the conspiracy. They need more information from me. I stopped at the ideal place. They will be desperate for the information soon. Then you get to look all skilful when you get the conspiracy kicked out. My gift to you, Simon."

Simon shook his head in disbelief at this self-delusional bearer of gifts. This was no gift. He was going to look like a monster not a hero. The amount of people he would have to convince that he was just doing his professional duty the day he represented William Hopper was going to amount to a job in itself. He raised his voice to Hopper.

"So you have no idea where she is do you? You were just making it up. Why? Do you enjoy it? Seeing her family upset? You have no idea the damage you are doing. I think you're fucking sick."

Simon was getting incensed now. Maybe enough of Hopper was still behind the line for Simon to translate his passion into violence. He had been used by a man who was just leading the poor family down a dead end. He was obviously loving every minute of it. Yet still he did not appear to be excited.

"Simon, you're getting too emotional. You have to focus. Soon I will need you more than I have so far."

Simon's voice was still raised significantly.

"Why? To tell them more lies?! What's this all about? Were you just bored in prison or something? Thought you'd have some fun?"

"It's always boring in prison. It gives you time to think. To reflect. To plan. Did you know that most major robberies are planned on association-time in prison? But they don't stop association do they? It's a human right isn't it? The right to associate? Just like it's a human right to be locked up for 23 out of every 24 hours. The Police need jobs don't they? That's why they don't abolish association. That's why crime persists. It's no good getting rid of it. What would you do for a living then Simon? You need people like me." He paused, for effect more than anything.

"Do you want to know what my plan was?"

Simon didn't say no. And he didn't get up. He found himself quite impressed, not in the positive sense that the word suggests but in the sense that he had never thought about Criminal Law in that way. Hopper was dead right. It is always rather unsettling to hear wisdom from those you consider the unwise. Hopper continued.

"I have a small radio in my cell. About eight o'clock last night I was listening to it. The news on every station had the same story. This girly that was snatched." He smiled.

"They were calling for witnesses, Simon. They probably still are. And as I lay there listening to it, imagining the fun that the men who took her were going to have with her I felt so jealous. Like when someone gets a bigger laugh from telling your joke than you did. But at the same time I really admired them, you know?"

Simon didn't know. How could anyone know? He felt his eyes well up slightly.

"I wanted to be a part of it. I wanted to be out there, free to…you know. I wished I could see a picture of her. See what they had got. My passion, Simon, it was like it was bigger than the cell I was in. I thought about it as I lay there. And it came to me. I know where she is. And then the next thought came to me – I can use that to get back out there. Back to my freedom."

Simon fought hard to control his anger. They never tell you what's in their heads unless they want you to mitigate for them. Why was he being so honest? Was he trying to shock him? If not he was doing it anyway. Simon had never had the door opened into the mind of a child-abuser before. They were just clients. You represent them and then go home and forget about them. But now he was being shown how real the perversion was. And he knew that what he had been told was only a small part of it. His voice was soft as he asked, "how do you know where she is?"

Hopper leant forward. His voice mirrored that of Simon's, soft and eerie. He looked Simon in the eye. Don't say it. Please don't say what I know you are going to say. Please don't let it be true. It was true.

"Because, Simon, she is in the same place we always take our children."

* * *

It had hit Simon like lightning. Sitting with him in a small grey cell was a man who was part of an organised group of child sex offenders. It was more real now. Hopper was part of a group who had abused clearly more than one child. He now knew why Hopper had threatened him with the Bar Council. He knew why he had refused to allow Caroline to be in the room with them. Now he was Hopper's to control. He knew exactly where the girl was. And he could tell them. He had obviously thought this through to the very end and Simon was now worried about the stage of the plan he found himself in. How much more was there?

"Now Simon I can see you are concerned. Don't be – we're almost finished now. There's just one problem left."

Simon could guess what it was.

"If I give the Police the location of the girl and my friends then the local Police of the area will be on the scene within an hour. When they find her they will find my friends too. And I can't have that Simon can I? I am sure you can imagine why."

"They want the names of the men Mr Hopper. They won't

budge on that."

"I expected so. They really don't play fair do they?"

Simon just sat in silence. There was nothing he could say to change anything now. He wondered how many children had been abused by the group. He couldn't get it out of his head. He just had to sit now and wait for Hopper to tell him what he wanted to do next.

"I was racking my brain about it last night. I was looking for a way to save the girly, my way out of here you see, but had to make sure my…friends…were safe too. You can see the dilemma I expect."

"Why are you so concerned about them?" Come on Hopper, just tell me where Hannah is.

Hopper leant forward, as it appeared he always did when making his more firm points.

"Because, Simon, the only person who knows where they are is me. They know that. They would also know that if they were caught I would be the reason why. And they would probably feel slightly aggrieved by that, don't you think?"

Simon seemed to agree from the look on his face. Perhaps agree is not an accurate reflection of how Simon felt. He could see the sense in Hopper's argument at least.

"And so I think it would be better for all concerned that they weren't on the scene when the Police arrive. But then – of course they will be there! It's in the middle of nowhere! And they have driven all the way up there to make sure they don't get disturbed. So finding her will mean finding them. And they will know I told the Police. They will think I set them up. They won't be happy about that Simon, no, they will be very upset."

"Are you afraid of them?"

Hopper looked like he was considering his answer rather than immediately dismissing whatever Simon like he had been doing so far, like his pupil-master tended to do most of the time.

"Not afraid of them, more afraid of what they would say. You see, Simon, I am part of the group. I have been there many times. I have taken part in the abduction, rape and killing of several girlies."

He didn't sound proud. He didn't sound ashamed. He just sounded like he was telling Simon about a very bland set of facts.

"If they think I set them up they will do the very same thing to me. They will tell the Police all of the things we have done together. I can't risk that."

Simon was now practical – it was a way of not facing up to the horror that he had just been exposed to. Horror that would probably dawn on him later on, at night, and prevent him from sleeping.

"Well I can't see them dropping the conspiracy if you won't give them names."

"Simon, you're right. Now I want you to listen very carefully to what I am about to say, because it needs to be done right. I'm going to give them the location and tell them that they will find everyone there. They will expect to rescue girly and make some arrests. But they won't. Well, girly will be rescued but no arrests will be made. You will have to go along with this – as far as you are concerned, everyone will be there, even though you know that they won't. In the meantime I will have to contact my friends and tell them to get out."

He looked up at Simon. This was the surprise he had in store for him. What he had been planning.

Simon asked Hopper a question knowing fully what the answer would be. But he wanted to make sure he was right. As though the seconds he took to ask the question would give him precious more time to be oblivious to what he was about to do.

"How can you contact them? they won't let you use a telephone in here!"

"No Simon they won't. That's why you will have to make the call."

★ ★ ★

Simon had seen it coming. Nothing seemed to surprise him now. Today was supposed to take five minutes. And now he found himself with little choice other than to mislead the Court. To compromise his professional standards. To effectively liberate someone who he knew would commit offence after offence against children for the rest of his life. He couldn't do it. Why couldn't someone else do it? He had to do it. No – there is another way surely. Find some other mug to do this. Simon was not going to put himself on the line for this man. He got up.

"You really are delusional. This just isn't the real world – I'm not bowing to you like that."

Hopper didn't even look at him.

"Simon, you're losing focus again. If you don't do what I ask then she will die. You could save her. Don't you want to? Do you want to explain to her family that their daughter is dead because you wouldn't make a phone call?"

"You're asking me to mislead the Court. You're asking me to pervert the course of justice. And I won't do it Hopper." He walked to the door.

"You've obviously made up your mind," said Hopper, though he knew he would be back.

SIXTEEN

The older man came into the room, having been woken by the larger man's shouting. They were all sitting at a table as he came in and to get to a seat, he walked past Hannah, placing his hand gently on her head as he did so.

"Hannah Taylor by the way," said the larger man.

"I heard," said the older man.

He sat down.

They were all eating bread and marmalade, Hannah included. The men were drinking coffee while Hannah had been given juice like the night before.

"Have you had the radio on?" asked the older man.

"No, not yet," replied the larger man.

The older man took a bite of some bread and walked over to the radio and turned it on.

He scanned through various stations, most of which were playing music. But he found a station that was half-way through a news bulletin eventually.

"...tor James Lowry described as well-built and in his 40s. Hannah's mother spoke to the media last night."

"Whoa, hang on," said the red-faced man, "turn it off a minute."

The older man looked puzzled, but did so.

"Girly, go and stand in the corner," the red-faced man continued.

He looked at them both as Hannah did as she was told.

"We don't want her hearing her mother's voice – she'll

never fucking shut up!"

The older man conceded.

"That's true – I'll listen to it through there," he said, nodding his head in the direction of the room in which he slept.

He left the room and turned up the volume as he walked into his bedroom. The report was almost over. There was no need to worry about the Police. The fact that an appeal was out meant that so far the Police had absolutely nothing. And so the older man was relieved. He heard Julie Taylor's words. "If you can see me – I love you."

Yes, but we love her too.

He walked back into the room.

"Nothing doing," he said as he placed the radio back where it had been.

The red-faced man had told Hannah they were going to play a game. And he had meant it too. But the other men had woken up by then. Now though, he did quite fancy a game of cards.

"Girly, do you know how to play cards?" he asked Hannah.

"No."

"Come round here then, you can be on my team."

She walked round and was placed on the red-faced man's lap; he held her there with his left arm around her waist.

The larger man picked up a pack of cards that were lying on the table – they had played a game or two last night after they had finished with Hannah. He dealt them out. They played for a while. Hannah even started to get used to the game. The red-faced man even let her pick which card he should play next, once she got the hang of it. She was starting to have fun playing the game. They were all laughing together now. She laughed too, sometimes. The larger man won the last hand. And the red-faced man threw his hand down on the table, smiling in defeat.

"Right," he said, lifting Hannah up from his lap and letting her onto the floor, "I've had enough of cards now."

He stood up and removed his sweater. He continued to undress. As did the other two men. And they raped her again.

SEVENTEEN

"Oh look at you all calm again!" said Hopper, as Simon came back into the conference cell.

Hopper had obviously never left the cell – he sat there finishing off some crisps that the officers had brought him, with some sandwiches and a cup of tea. He must have told the officers that Simon was coming straight back. That was presumptuous – indicating an arrogance that was irritating though not surprising. After all, here Simon was, back in the cells. He would not usually put up with this sort of behaviour. But what could he do? He had to endure Hopper's bullshit because there was a wider issue here. Today wasn't about Simon. He looked at the big picture, the one involving a kidnapped four year-old girl.

There is a certain calmness when one accepts a lack of choice. There was no way around this problem – Hopper had counted on this, that he could use and abuse Simon's sense of humanity against him. Simon was calm. He just wanted to get it over with. He wanted to go home. But he wanted to save the girl too. At least someone in this room cared in the slightest what had become of her. He sighed as he looked at Hopper.

"Explain something to me," he said.

Hopper looked up and raises his eyebrows earnestly

"How can you be sure she is still alive? If they find a body then I don't think they will honour any deal they have made with you."

Hopper laughed at Simon. As though surprised at his

ignorance. As though pitying his naivety.

"Of course she's still alive! Why the hell would they want to kill her yet? After all that effort! Come on Simon, you really should think before you speak!"

Simon was pleased to be patronised. At least he knew Hannah was still alive.

"So you mean she isn't in any danger?"

Now that *was* naïve.

"Well I wouldn't go that far Simon – she's certainly in danger. Just not for a few more days that's all."

"What do you mean?"

"OK. They took her and drove for a long time. It's just not worth the bother to kill them for a few days at least."

Simon started to feel his stomach churn now. It was as though Hopper was talking about an animal.

"I don't understand. I mean you hear about, you know, children on the news. Them being found murdered."

"Yes – they are the ones taken by disorganised people. We, on the other hand, have quite a good thing going on up there."

It was Hopper's apparent pride that sickened and frightened Simon more than anything. He wondered how many more there must have been. How many more there would inevitably be if Hopper got out. He was obviously part of a sophisticated group – one that was to be treated with extreme caution. They must have been doing this for years.

There is some evil that it suffices to merely despise but then there is evil that demands respect and must be taken seriously. This man was far above Simon's imaginings. Like he was part of a reality Simon was unaware of until today. He felt belittled by it. Embarrassed. Out of his depth at the very least. But it was his reality. He was on his own. And in this job, you don't get a note from mummy. Hopper continued.

"When we take our girlies to the house we are safe – it

really is in the middle of nowhere. No-one ever goes there. That's how organised we are! It gives us at least a week before we have to come back down to Newcastle. Christ, we've even got a phone line installed!"

Simon didn't want to know the answer to what he was about to ask.

"What happens to the girls?"

"Well they are killed, obviously."

Simon almost vomited. He could feel himself about to retch, so matter-of-fact was the attitude of this monster.

"You have to get rid of them really. They would only go and talk. Maybe not straight away, but eventually."

"How many times have you done it?" Simon asked, visibly trying to restrain the tears that were ready to fall.

"Don't trouble yourself with details like that Simon. I am only telling you what you need to know. I want you understand me. What we are and why we do it."

"I don't want to understand you. I don't need to know about you."

"Of course you do. You want to know because it sickens you. You want to cry – I can see it. But you couldn't leave the conversation like this. You're too curious."

"What is it they say – curiosity killed the cat?"

"Simon that's just a phrase invented by someone who wanted nosey people to leave him alone. This is your chance to get inside my mind. And I need you to hate me so much that you will apply your mind to what I have asked you to do. I demand efficiency and only your abhorrence will guarantee me that from you."

"Then tell me why you kill children."

"I've told you! They talk! It's no good living your life waiting for a child to grow up and start talking. You can't live like that – you'd go mad!" Hopper laughed. As though what he was saying was an accepted fact. Like murder was justified as it allowed the men a sense of peace and finality.

"These girlies you hear about on the news, which you really shouldn't trust by the way, are killed because they are a risk. They would expose whoever took them. It is really the only solution. They promise they won't tell, but they always do."

Simon really wanted that note from his mother now. He began to think of her. What would she think of today? Would she feel he was doing the right thing? Would she even think he was in the right job? Would she understand that his hands were tied? Perhaps only she would. It's hard to convince people that you are only doing your job. Especially when you can't actually tell them anything without going against your own professional codes of conduct. Hopper went on.

"Why do you think people who do it to their own children don't get rid of them?"

Simon looked blankly. He didn't know the answer. How could he? He had never even thought to ask himself the question in the first place.

"It's because they need them. Our girlies don't need us. They can live without us. But children need their parents. Or step-parents. Or the people who work in the foster homes they live in. What are they without these people? Fucking nothing, Simon, that's what. That's why they don't tell anyone. There's too much to lose. This is very basic stuff Simon."

Simon felt as though he was being told off. Like he owed Hopper knowledge. Hopper seemed to be judging him for not knowing about this topic, but Simon took comfort from the fact that he had never needed to wonder about it. He had never experienced any form of abuse from his parents. His experience of child abductions was limited to news bulletins and programmes dedicated to true-life crimes.

"You are wondering whether I do it to my own children

aren't you Simon?"

"I didn't know you had children," said Simon. He didn't realise he was crying until this point but as he felt a tear fall from his jaw and land on the lapel of his jacket he knew that he must be. Such was the numbness of his face – the place to which Hopper's words were being directed. And while he felt a wave of compassion and pity for the children of this man, he couldn't help but think they were still Hopper's children, tarnished and perhaps as poisonous as he was.

"Of course I do," Hopper said with a slight smile.

Hopper's smile grew as Simon got up and left the room. He knew he had really got to him. And by simply telling him the truth.

EIGHTEEN

The older man walked back into the room, having put Hannah back in downstairs.

"Did you notice how much it stinks in that room?" he asked the others.

The larger man had not been in yet. He was listening to the radio again. Still nothing.

"Yeah – it's pretty bad," replied the red-faced man.

"We should do something about it. It'll just get worse," said the older man as both of them looked to the larger man.

"I'll have a look later," said the larger man.

"Well why don't we just have a look now?" asked the older man.

"I said I'll look later! We don't need to worry about it for a few days yet."

In the room where Hannah sat, freezing and sore, was a latch door set into the floor at the far end. She hadn't seen it, with it being so dark.

The door led down into a basement room which the three men, and a fourth, had dug out themselves several years before, when the older man looked younger and the larger man was slimmer. Underneath the floor of the basement room was evidence of their cunning. Proof that they were organised.

"How many are down there now anyway?" asked the red-faced man.

"Eight I think," said the larger man, still fiddling with the radio.

"Well if it smells like that now we may well have to think about doing another room out," said the older man.

The larger man was getting more irritated.

"What the hell for?! Who's going to notice the smell? You only smell it when you go in."

There was no telling him when he was like this. They let it go. He was probably right anyway.

Hannah wasn't crying. She was just sitting as she had been before breakfast. She still didn't understand, and now she was even more confused. In the minutes before they had hurt her again, they had all been having fun. They had laughed. She had laughed too.

She thought of her parents. And Daniel. She really wished they were here to help her. To make her understand what was happening to her.

There was no particular reason why she decided to investigate the room. She knew she probably wouldn't be able to get out. But she wanted to know more about where she was. She was in a questioning mood. Why were they doing this? Why were they happy and then angry? Where was she? She crawled around on the floor, feeling the walls as she went. She eventually felt the big door where the men came in to collect her and knew that there was only one more wall to feel around before she was back to where she started. At least now she had an idea of how big the room was. She stood up now. She walked around, with her hands out in case there was something to bump into. After a while she felt something on the floor. It creaked and didn't feel as cold as the concrete. She knelt down and felt around it. It was like a door. But in the floor.

There was a handle in the door. She turned it instinctively. It wasn't even all that heavy to lift. So she did. And the smell almost knocked her over. She dropped the door back down again as she covered her nose and eyes. It landed with a loud crash, an indication not of the weight of the door but of the silence of Hannah's surroundings. The men heard it and came running down the stairs.

They piled in. The larger man shone a torch at Hannah. And he looked at the door, now back where it was. But with the handle turned to allow it to be opened. He knew what the noise had been, as did the others.

The older man walked over to her and lifted her up. She was sure that she was going to be hurt again for what she had done. But the older man didn't hurt her. He just smiled and said "Not yet, girly."

The larger man opened the latch for himself, winced and closed it again. God it is rancid isn't it?

NINETEEN

Simon left the cell area and went straight upstairs. There were people everywhere, coming and going. This was not the place for someone who wanted to be on their own. He really needed to be alone right now. He needed this all to just go away. He needed that which Hopper had told him not to be true. But he knew that every word of it was true. He walked into the toilet. At least there was no-one in there. He looked in the mirror and realised that he still had his wig on. He took it off.

He looked at his reflection. He began to think of the days when he was studying. Days when he would never have imagined this sort of case. He thought of his pupillage days when he constantly told himself that he would one day show Donald Ramsey just how good he was. What would Donald say to him right now? He would probably have told him to withdraw. But Simon couldn't withdraw. He would never forgive himself if he had wasted time because if Hannah Taylor was found murdered he would never truly know how much of a role he had played in it. He had inherited this situation. It was not of his creation. But it was given to him to deal with and he had to do the right thing. This was more important than a colourful speech to a Jury. More important than a pat on the back from a gangland client who would tell him he needn't worry about paying for a drink in town ever again. He splashed some water on his face and thought about the poor girl and what must be happening to her.

John Davis walked into the toilets.

"Ah, Simon," he said as he took a place at a urinal, "I hear you're having troubles."

Simon didn't like talking to people while they were busy answering the call of nature. But then it was a triviality to be reserved for a time when things were bland. It didn't matter today. He didn't turn round. But he spoke.

"You could say that."

"Well that's the name of the game my friend, the name of the game."

"I know. I just want today to be over. Fucking client is killing me."

Davis could see that Simon wasn't just saying words. He was feeling them.

"Alan told me about this chap, Hopper," he said as he came over to wash his hands, "are you managing?"

"Yeah, it'll work itself out. I just want to go home, John."

Davis looked at him and flicked the water from his hands. Best to let him get on with it. Davis didn't give advice unless someone asked for it and that was one of the reasons that Simon got on with him.

"You poor sod."

Simon gave a half-smile in agreement.

"You'll be ok. Ring me later tonight if you want to. Anyway, must dash ok?"

"Yeah."

Davis was right. Simon was a poor sod. He wished he could trade places with Davis. But then he wouldn't wish Hopper on anyone. That would be criminal itself.

Simon left the toilet and walked into the advocates' dining room. Caroline was sitting reading a book. She saw him and put it down.

"Hi Simon – what's happening?"

"Oh, just plodding on. He's going to tell them some more

when he feels like it."

"Why didn't he want me there anyway? He's not trying to trap you is he?"

"He wouldn't dare."

He would. In fact he had.

"Well, just be careful."

"Yeah," Simon said and paused, "it's a good job you brought something to read."

He couldn't tell Caroline what Hopper was making him do. He didn't want anyone to know. He wished that he could tell her. Someone. But it was a secret for Hopper and he only. She went back to reading her book. Simon thought about getting them both a coffee and sitting down for a few minutes. But he couldn't. He had to go back downstairs and face the reality of what he felt may well be his last ever case.

TWENTY

Hopper had his feet up on the table this time. He still hadn't been back to his cell. And although that had been Simon's suggestion to the security staff, Hopper's own arrogance would probably have meant that they allowed him to remain in the conference cell anyway.

"Had a breather?"

"Yeah, just needed to go to the loo"

"No you didn't Simon, don't lie to me. You're a fucking timewaster. I saw your face when you got up and left. What business is it of yours how I raise my children? Eh? It's not about you, this. It's about me. And this fucking girly you're all so bothered about."

Simon felt the remarks hit him and just bounce off. They didn't make him jump anymore now. His revulsion had peaked and comments like that about Hannah made no marginal difference to him. Hopper was right though, this was about Hannah. And Simon now began to wonder what effect his temporary departure might have had on the chances of finding her alive.

"Just tell me what I need to do to save her."

Hopper took his feet off the table and sat properly.

"Now you're giving me what I want you see? It really is better for everyone you know. Even a dirty old man like me!"

Simon felt that a reply to the effect of 'you're no kind of man' would sound a bit contrived. But he was tempted.

"Well?"

"OK Simon, it's nearly the end now. The Police know that my friends drove up through Moorfoot but I stopped there because there are a thousand roads to choose from after that. Once you've made the call I will tell you the rest and they can go and retrieve girly. Get your pen out."

Simon did as instructed. And Hopper dictated a telephone number to him.

"Now when you speak to him, he'll be very nervous. He gets like that. Very professional, you know, likes to think he's totally aware. So you will have to tell him as soon as you ring that you are calling on my behalf. Refer to me as 'Uncle Billy'".

Simon was taking it all in. And he was praying for a way out. Now that the time was about to come, he knew he couldn't do it. Even with what was at stake.

"Tell him what's happened. That I have found a way out. And tell them to get their skates on. Because you'll be telling the Judge where they are as soon as you are done with the call. Simon, it won't be Northumbria Police that go looking for her, it will be local Scottish Police."

"So they're definitely in Scotland?"

Hopper stopped.

"Oooh, good one, I forgot I hadn't told you that for definite," he smiled, "anyway, it won't take them long to get there, especially if they use the helicopter. So they will have to pack up and leave as soon as you put the phone down."

Simon sat in silence, looking at Hopper.

"Simon, I hope you are listening to this. Don't mess this up because I have your career in my hands. I can start telling stories whenever I want to."

Ideas had a habit of popping into Simon's head from time to time. Just like they had yesterday when he was cross-examining the officer in charge of the Walton case. And another one popped into his head there and then in the cells as he was

135

receiving Hopper's edict. And he felt a wave of adrenaline.

The thought of merely pretending to Hopper that he had made the call had occurred to him. By the time Hopper had found out, Hannah would be back home. And he considered doing it. But he couldn't. For a simple reason. Once Hopper did find out, he would have a trump card to play on Simon. His career in his hands, as he had said. Simply reporting him to the Bar Council. Simon would be disbarred. No question.

But another idea had since popped into Simon's head. A better idea. Oh my God Hopper I am going to fucking get you for this. Enjoy your patronising while you can.

TWENTY ONE

"There's nowhere else to put her," said the older man.

"Alright, but I don't want her near that latch door. Not for a few days anyway," said the larger man, "go and get that rope from the car."

The older man went outside and fetched a length of rope from the boot of the Sharan. Hopper had always kept rope in the car, none of them had known why. Maybe it was another example of why he was the principal member of the group. Always prepared. The larger man had assumed this position while the group were a man down, but he would never have thought to carry rope with him.

He returned moments later.

"Right, we'll take her back down," said the larger man.

They made her lie down on the floor of the cold room while they searched for something to tie her to. There was nothing at all in the room. Eventually, the red-faced man spoke. And the other men agreed.

"Girly, lie down on your front," said the larger man.

She did so without question.

The larger man bent her legs back towards her head and tied her arms and legs together behind her back. It was beyond uncomfortable but still she made no sound. Any hint of a fight had left her now. Yet she did not think about home. She had accepted the fact that she was alone, with three men hurting her whenever they felt like it. Even after having been nice to her. Giving her food. Playing a game.

She lay there on her front, on the cold, dirty floor. In total silence. And waited to be released. Although now she knew that release would only come at the price of being hurt again. She knew it was only a matter of time before release came. The men had taken her in order to hurt her. She knew that now. She knew they would be doing it again and again.

* * *

Simon Silver had left the cell area now, carrying a piece of paper with a telephone number on it. And he had to find a payphone. There were only two in Court. And people would be coming and going. He could not let anyone hear what he was going to say. He had doubts again. He couldn't do this. He was committing an offence. Simple as that. There was no way that he could allow himself to do that. It was against everything he had been taught. Never compromise your professional standards to please someone. Never do anything that might bring the Bar into disrepute.

He left the Court building, stood outside and sighed. There was no way to win this one. If he did as Hopper had asked then Hopper would be released. Did this mean that children who would otherwise grow old having never been abused would now be unable to grow old at all? Of course it did. He could do this again. The four men together might take child after child. And Simon would be a part of it.

But if he didn't do it, what then? Hopper would surely be convicted of the conspiracy with his taped confession. And he would languish in prison with nothing better to do than to ruin Simon's career. But at least he would never kidnap and murder another child. He could just pretend to have made the call. But then the men would be arrested. And they would think Hopper had set them up. And they would tell all. Hopper would be back in prison anyway, getting his own back on Simon in the same way.

Hannah was the priority. It was all about her, as Hopper had said. He could save her. He would tell the men not to do anything to her. She would survive. She would be rescued. She would be back with her family, ready to live whatever life she could now be said to have.

He had to make the call. There was no other way. But there was another angle to the bargain. There was a way of making sure that all four men were in prison without further risk to Hannah. Simon's heart jumped when he realised it. But it meant doing something beyond unprofessional.

★ ★ ★

The three men had gone back up to the room where the rapes had taken place. That is where they heard the telephone ring. They stood in silence as it did so. It just rang and rang. The older man looked at the larger man, who in turn looked at the red-faced man. Who the hell was that?

"Shit – who the hell knows this number?" asked the larger man.

"Maybe it's a wrong number," suggested the older man.

"Fucking better be – do you think I should answer it?"

"I don't know."

Hopper would know. Hopper. Maybe it was him.

The larger man looked nervous for the first time since the other two men could remember. They didn't blame him though – they were nervous too.

"What if it's Billy?" he asked.

"Answer it," said the red-faced man.

"What if it isn't?" asked the older man.

It rang on and on.

The larger man walked to the phone and looked at the other two men as he put his hand on the receiver in order to pick it up. Were they sure? Were they all agreed?

"Hello?"

"I'm ringing for Uncle Billy"

"Who's this?"

"Never mind who it is. Just listen."

Silence. The other two men came to the phone to see if they could hear anything.

"Hopper is about to tell the Police where you are," said Simon.

Shit. More silence.

Simon sensed the reason for the pause in the conversation. They were obviously freaked out. But what if this man hung up? What would happen to Hannah? He had to reassure this man.

"Look – don't worry, he won't say a word until he knows that I have spoken to you. He has it all worked out. Now look, you have to leave where you are right now. Seriously. Go right now. And leave Hannah there. Alive. He won't be released if Hannah is dead. That's the little girl's name."

"I know. Hannah Taylor"

Good, at least he's talking.

"Right. The Police will be there in minutes – literally – after they find out the location so you will have to pack up and go straight away. I don't know exactly where you are myself, because Hopper hasn't told even me yet…"

Come on, Simon, don't give them clues as to who you are.

"…but wherever it is, I know that there are a lot of country roads there, so you'll have to decide yourself which is the best way to go."

"Alright," said the larger man. He knew that they had to leave and they had to do it now. Hopper had made that decision for them. He told them when he was arrested he would find a way to get out. This was obviously it. But he was telling them in advance to get out. So he wasn't setting them up. He obviously knew what he was doing and that's why the larger man followed the instructions without question.

"We have to go," he said as he turned to the other men.

"What? Why? What's happened?" asked the older man, nervously.

"Hopper's told the Police where we are."

"What?!"

The older man became incensed, and ran into the kitchen. He rarely reacted. But then he was rarely scared. He was scared now.

"Where are you going?" asked the larger man.

"I'm getting the fucking knife!"

He grabbed a knife and ran downstairs. Into the cold room.

They talk, he thought. You have to stop them, he thought. Not that it will do any good once the Police get here. They will find them. All eight of them. And this new one. Better dead and silent than alive and talking. Little bitch.

The other men were running down the stairs after him. But he had a good head start on them. He barged into the cold room. Hannah was still lying on her front, her legs and arms still tied as they were. She couldn't have moved anyway. She wouldn't move now. She might try to wriggle. But it would do no good. It was the best option. There was in fact no other. They talk.

He lunged towards Hannah, holding the knife in his hand.

"I'm going to fucking cut you, you little bitch!"

It was perhaps more frightening that Hannah didn't make a sound.

"NO!!!" shouted the larger man, entering the cold room a

second or two later. He stopped by the entrance to the room. The older man put the knife to Hannah's throat and she remained without reaction, save for a slight welling-up in her eyes. This was the man who had carried her. Who had brought her food and juice. But who had raped her. And now held a cold blade to her throat.

"He says we have to leave her!"

The older man still held the knife where it was, rested against Hannah's throat. Ready to solve the talking problem.

"What?" he asked, his eyes still firmly on the girl he was about to kill.

"The guy on the phone! Look, think about it – he said Hopper won't get out unless she stays alive. He must have a plan worked out."

"But she can describe us! I'm going to fucking do it."

"I know she can, but that's Hopper's error. We can sort it later. Move to a new area. We've done it before. If he stays in prison he can describe us too – they'll make him a deal, you know they will. He's done what he's done. He must know what he's doing."

That part at least made sense to the older man. It was that sentence that saved Hannah's life.

He passed the knife to the larger man. And grabbed Hannah by the throat. He whispered to her with force. Her entire body shook as he did so.

"If you fucking talk to anyone about us we will take you again. And we will hurt you even more. We will do it to your mother. And your brother. You little fucking bitch, girly, you never ever talk about us!"

They closed the door behind them and locked it. Hannah was still there, on her front. Freezing cold and dirty. In total darkness. And total silence once more.

TWENTY TWO

"Well?" asked Hopper.

"I made the call."

"Good man. Thought maybe you would have second thoughts."

"I did – lots of second thoughts. But I care about that little girl."

Hopper laughed.

"And yet you're going to unleash me on the public again! That's a funny thing isn't it? You know what might happen don't you? Are you scared?" He smiled at Simon. "Don't forget what I've got on you now Simon. I could crucify you. You make sure you behave yourself. This is our secret and it will stay that way. No-one else needs to know about it. It would just cause problems. For both of us. Never forget that."

Simon wanted to do all sorts of things. Launch himself at Hopper. Hit him over and over. Break down crying like a baby. He sat still. For all of his life, Simon had needed to do this job. It was all he could do. There was no motivation for anything else. It was the Bar or unemployment. His dream. His father's dream for him too. They had shared this ambition. Anyone can make someone do something. But you know you have inspired someone if you can make them *want* to do something. Simon had wanted to do this for as long as he could remember. And now he was in the company of someone who could take it away from him whenever he felt like it. What would his father think of him now? He had not thought about his father until this moment. It seems he only thought of him when things got rough. He never received praise from his father and no longer sought to impress him. But he could imagine him there in the room, looking disappointed. Oh Simon, what have you done? You've let me down, you really have. God, why are you like this? Perhaps inspired is an inaccurate way to describe Simon's motivation to do this job. It was more like he was proving to his father that he could do it. Still waiting for him to say 'well done'.

Why the hell did I make that call? Anything else could have been explained away. They would never believe Hopper over me if he claimed I was representing him when I knew he was guilty. But I have done the one thing that he can get me for. There is no other way to explain why the men weren't there when the Police arrived. If Hopper tells them I made the call they will look into it. And I used a payphone. Oh God. They can trace it. Shit. Dad, help me for God's sake.

But Simon was on his own. With a man that had inspired him to want to make that call. And he really did want to. Because it was the right thing to do. People would understand wouldn't they? He would be dis-barred of course, but no-one would hate him. All this unfinished business with his father had led Simon to forget the idea he had had before he made the call. And when the realisation came back to him he felt the rush of adrenaline again. And he looked up at Hopper. No need to fear him at all. He had plans of his own.

"Well, William, I'm not likely to tell anyone am I? I'm not going to damage my own career!"

The first time he had called him William. Simon thought back to earlier in the day, when Hopper had called him Simon for the first time. When he had put his plans into action. Now Simon was doing the same. Their little secret? Simon wondered how many times he had said that. To children. It *would* be a secret. Because what he had in mind would mean that Hopper would want to maintain silence too.

OK Hopper, start talking. Then I will start my own little game.

"Now then, Simon. Have you ever been up that way yourself? Lammermuir and Moorfoot? It's very nice up there."

"No, I have never been. I've been up to Edinburgh but never that way."

"Well you wouldn't, there's nothing there really. That's why I chose it you see."

"You mean the place where they took Hannah?"

"Yes, I found it."

Silence. What do want – praise?

"Anyway, we take them to an old quarry. There are some houses there, mostly derelict but one of them is habitable. To an extent anyway."

"And that's where she is?"

"Yes, she will be in a ground floor room. There's a latch door in the floor there, which leads to a basement where we put them when we leave."

Simon knew what that meant. And he did well not to let it get to him. He did even better to ask the next question.

"Well, why didn't you get me to tell them to move her from that room? They'll find the bodies of the girls."

"Ooh – look at you, getting the hang of things! Actually, Simon, I did think about that but to be honest they will check the place out anyway so it would make no difference. And what's more, how are they going to know I was involved? It's not like you're going to tell them is it?!"

Simon laughed.

"No – I don't really fancy queuing up to cash my giro every Thursday thanks very much!"

Hopper was right to think that Simon wouldn't tell anyone.

He also thought Simon was totally on his side now. That he was indeed malleable. But Hopper was wrong to think that.

"So how do you get there?" asked Simon.

"Well, that's the tricky bit, which is why I think they'll send a helicopter first. My friends only know the road that gets them there and so they will take that road back. That's OK though, because the helicopter will arrive from the other direction and won't see them."

"God, you really are organised aren't you?"

"Very. You have to be, really. My…condition forces me to be."

"But what if they tie you to the murders?"

"They won't."

"How can you be sure?"

"Because they don't have my DNA profile. Or that of my friends. Nor will they ever when you think about it. Like you say, you won't tell anyone will you?!"

"I can't tell anyone. I would end up in prison."

"That's right Simon. You would do well to always remember that. No job. A prison sentence. And think about all the people you have prosecuted over the years. I'm sure they would love to see you in prison with them!"

Simon would never tell anyone. He couldn't. But not for the reason Hopper thought. If there was no other way to bring the four men to justice then perhaps he would toy with the idea of sacrificing his own career. It would be quite a soul-searching thing to do. But there was no need. There was another way. Simon would keep his job too. As long as Hopper thought he was on his side.

But that was not the case of course. And what Simon had in mind amounted to a grave offence too. Academically, Simon was probably accountable for any foreseeable consequence that came from it. And you didn't need a crystal ball to foresee what would happen. Perhaps that's why despite the adrenaline rush, Simon did wonder whether he could go through with it.

The whole affair was coming full-circle now. His revulsion had allowed Hopper what he wanted. The phone call. Maybe Simon needed to be reminded of his abhorrence. Perhaps only that would guarantee that he went through with his own plan. He should have had enough so far. He knew what this man was. He knew what he had done. But Simon needed one final push.

"How many girls are there?" he asked in an almost whispered voice.

"Oh I don't know – eight or so? That sounds about right."

Eight children. Eight families whose lives were ruined, cut short perhaps, by the perversion of four men. And there would be no justice for them. They would never know. They would walk down the street and wonder if they were passing the person who killed their daughter. No justice for these innocent families. Families who were to be admired by anyone fortunate enough not to have ever been harmed. Or see anyone they loved harmed. How could these people survive? While I have been studying, working, spending money on fast cars and restaurant meals, these people have been crying themselves to sleep. They are so far above me. I really am nothing compared to them. I would crack, but they survive. Because of you, Hopper, and your kind. You are the author of that. The world is dying because of people like you. You told me that you needed me to hate you. Now I agree with you. You were in control when you said that. Now I am in control. You have inspired me. That's enough hatred now. You have made me want to finish you. To deliver justice. And now I have to do one final piece of acting. I need you to think that you impress me.

"Eight? Fucking hell, William, you've gone unnoticed the whole time?"

Hopper smiled.

"That's right Simon. All these years."

"So what should I tell the Judge? Alan Riley will be in Chambers too and he will have to tell the Police straight away."

"Yes I know. The place to find girly is the detached house at the Calder Pit. It's not on any modern maps so you'll have to tell them to look at an old one. The Police in Scotland will probably be able to find it. Especially if they use a helicopter because they will see the quarry from the air."

"Calder Pit, OK," said Simon, making a note.

"So off you go then. Go and tell the Judge. Get me out of this cell!"

* * *

There was no respectful smile from Lowry, Austin or Whelan. Simon would probably never get one. Alan and Simon walked back into Court and broke with convention by not asking Charles if they could see him in Chambers. He had told them just to come straight through and when they knocked on the door it was opened immediately.

"So what's the situation?" asked Charles.

"Well, I have a location Judge," said Simon.

Charles sat down and invited the Bar to follow suit.

Simon knew that the day was almost over as far as he was concerned. Once he told Charles about the Calder Pit his work was done. Well, not quite, but his official work was done at least. But he needed Hopper to be released. That was vital. It was going to look dangerous and he couldn't tell them why he had to be released. They would just have to accept that he was being professional. He wouldn't want to bring his own professional conduct rules into it, but if he did he knew that he could argue that he was doing the best for his client and not being swayed by a third party. That's what the rules say. Interpreting them is matter for whoever is arguing the point.

"Judge, before I disclose it I would like to take this opportunity to make a representation on behalf of the Defendant."

"Go on," said Charles.

"Once I have disclosed the name of the place where Hannah will be found, the Police will no doubt liaise with Officers in Scotland who will carry out the rescue. Once that is done she will be brought back here and be returned to her family. You will both, I hope, remember earlier today when we sat in these very chairs and I told you that Hopper wanted certain guarantees?"

"I remember, Simon. He wants to be released and go to a new address."

"Yes, Judge. Now we discussed earlier that this would only happen on the proviso that Hannah was found alive. I have no doubt that she will be and so I am flagging this up now since it will be you, Judge, that will have to release him in open Court."

Charles sighed.

"Yes I will won't I? And I will no doubt make it into the national papers eventually."

"Perhaps we all will, Judge"

"Well, tomorrow's fish and chip paper – isn't that what they say?" said Charles.

There was a silence.

"It's OK," continued Charles, "I've been thinking about it all day. Today has been nothing if not exciting. Better than a list of pleas and sentences. Which is pretty much my day-to-day routine!"

Simon had not thought about Charles having any second thoughts. But it seemed as though he didn't have any.

"Well it's a routine that we all aspire to," said Simon, lying through his teeth.

"So where is she Simon?" asked Charles.

"Do I take it that I have the guarantee?"

"Yes, Simon. He will be released once I am informed of Hannah's safety."

"Thank you Judge. She is in a place called the Calder Pit. There are apparently some houses there and one which is detached. That's the house in which she is being held."

Simon knew that she was no longer being held as such. The kidnappers would be on their way back to England now. She was there, but they weren't. And no-one had noticed that yet. What would he say if they did notice? More gambling no doubt.

"Where is this Calder Pit?" asked Alan, speaking for the first time.

"Well, you'll need to get an old map to find it. But I was thinking that if the Officers in Scotland used a helicopter then they will find it."

"So – you don't actually know how to get there do you Simon?" asked Charles.

"Judge, it may well be that the Defendant doesn't know either. He didn't give me directions. But he said the Scots Police will be able to see it from the air because there is an old quarry there."

"That's not enough I'm afraid," said Charles.

Oh God this isn't going to work. And I need him released.

Life works itself out from time to time. Sometimes surprising things take place. Simon would never have imagined that Alan Riley would help him out. Especially after his performance this morning over the purpose for including the conspiracy count in the first place. But he did help.

"Judge, it seems to me that while we wait for exact directions we may be wasting valuable time. The Scots Police will know more than we do – it won't take them long I don't suppose. They could even direct the helicopter while it's in the air."

Simon felt adrenaline again. His problem was sorted out now.

"I suppose so. OK then – Alan you may as well go and talk to the Officer in the case now. Simon, you need to speak to Hopper. You will probably have told him this already but the Court will require an address from him. We will need to know where he's going before we release him. If he behaves himself then he needn't worry about getting arrested. And you can tell him that from me. But Simon I need an address."

Simon hadn't told Hopper about that. But Charles didn't need to know that.

"Will do," said Simon, getting up.

The Bar left Judge's Chambers. The Bench had yet another cup of coffee.

* * *

"Well, it's done," said Simon.

"Good. So what's happening now?" asked Hopper.

"Alan Riley will be telling the coppers about the Calder Pit and then I daresay they will send word to Scotland."

"So I pulled it off," said Hopper, sitting back in his chair, "never a doubt though Simon. It had success written all over it!"

"Well there's one more thing to think about. The Judge wants to know where you're going to go before he releases you. I need an address from you."

Hopper sat bolt upright again and Simon thought he knew why. He continued.

"I know I should really have thought about that before, but to be honest you had my mind on other things."

"Oh it's fine Simon. I knew they would want an address. Anyway, I had one ready cos if I didn't have somewhere to go then my idea wouldn't have worked. See how prepared I am? More prepared than you are, obviously."

Oh, I don't know about that, Hopper.

"So where is it?"

"I have a property in Nottingham which I rent out. But it's been empty for a few months so I'll go there."

"What about your children?"

"I know, and my wife. You'd think I wouldn't want to leave them behind wouldn't you? Well, Simon, between you and me, I don't really intend to stay there for very long. I'll stay there a few days so the Police think I'm there. And then I will float away. I'll have changed my name by then anyway. Maybe I'll call myself Simon."

Oh, I don't think it'll come to that.

"And the family can move somewhere else with me. I quite fancy Scotland actually."

No, it definitely won't come to that.

Hopper wrote the new address on a piece of paper that Simon had handed to him. And then got up.

"Now you hold your tongue, Simon. Remember what I can do. I've got you by the balls. Don't make me squeeze them."

Hopper left the conference cell. And Simon sat for a while, before heading upstairs wondering how far Caroline had got in her book.

TWENTY THREE

Lowry was sitting in CPS room drinking coffee, with his tie loosened perhaps to soften the headache that the cup of coffee was going to worsen. Austin and Whelan sat in silence on either side of him. Alan Riley walked in.

"I have a location," he said.

Lowry shot up.

"Where?"

"In Scotland. An old quarry called the Calder Pit. But you will need to liaise with the Scottish Police because we have no idea how to get to it by road. Hopper apparently only knows the way by sight. He says, well in fact it was Simon Silver who told me, but anyway you will have to tell them to go there by helicopter. Apparently it's on older maps but should be visible by air."

It was another case of Lowry not allowing himself to get too excited. He was close now, but yet again Hopper had held back on something. In truth he had told Simon everything he knew and Simon had passed the message on accurately. But Lowry was not a man easily swayed by blind faith. He dealt in hard facts. And ninety-nine per cent was not enough to allow him to start celebrating. In addition, he had no contacts in Scotland at all.

"I'm going outside to get a decent signal," he said.

"What do you want us to do Jim?" asked Austin.

"Nothing. Just wait there. I will be back in a minute."

Lowry wanted this for himself. That's why he had left his

two companions in the CPS room. And that's why he cursed the fact he would have to ring Helen Wilde.

"Jim?"

"Yes ma'am. We have a location for the girl. It's in south-west Scotland."

"Well done, Jim. Thanks for letting me know."

"Ma'am there's something else."

"Oh?"

"I don't know anyone in Scotland. I wondered if you did. It will be quicker for Police in Scotland to find her."

"OK Jim, leave it with me, I will make a few calls. Er...what's best? Tell you what, I'll get someone from Scotland to ring you for instructions once I've spoken to them. Where is the place by the way?"

"The Calder Pit apparently. An old quarry."

"Oh – well I've no idea where that is. Just sit tight and wait for someone in Scotland to ring you."

"Thanks ma'am."

The line went dead. And Lowry walked back upstairs.

★ ★ ★

Simon walked up to Caroline. She was still sitting at the same table as she was earlier. Still reading.

"Well, Caroline, it's pretty much done."

She put down her book.

"Really? What's happened? Did they find the girl?"

"No, not yet. Hopper's given them the location and they're going to get in touch with Officers in Scotland. So I suppose it's just a question of waiting," he replied as he sat down.

There was a silence as Simon searched for something to say. He couldn't think of anything at all. He would pretend that it was, but in truth his silence was not due to the day's events.

He just had no idea of what to say to her. And so he gave up.

"You can go home if you want you know, there's nothing more to do here than just hang around."

"Oh it's OK – actually, I wouldn't mind waiting here to see what happens to be honest."

Excellent.

"Well, just be ready to wait for a good while."

And then I can give you a lift back. Maybe we will stop off for a drink. Maybe we can stay out all night and get to know each other.

"It's fine, I'm quite into this book anyway. And I'll call my boyfriend and get him to pick me up a bit later."

Boyfriend. Yeah, thought so.

"Well, whatever's best. Look – I'm going through into the lounge so I'll see you up at Court. They'll put a call out," he said, getting up.

"OK see you in a bit," she replied without looking up at him.

★ ★ ★

Lowry stayed outside. His heart was beating fast. It was a cold day, not that he really noticed. It was a good ten minutes before his mobile phone rang. It seemed longer than that.

"Is that Jim Lowry?"

"Yes?"

"Jim, it's Joe Makin from Strathclyde Police . I've just had a call from Helen Wilde who told me to contact you. Is this about the girl on the news?"

"Yes it is. Look, we know where she is and I was hoping you could organise the rescue."

"What's the location?"

Lowry told Makin about the Calder Pit. A helicopter was

organised and a promise was made that all efforts would be poured into finding it quickly. Lowry went back to waiting.

Whelan took the opportunity to ask a question that had been bugging him.

"Jim – can I ask you something?"

"Uh-huh."

"Well, you know the interview I typed up?"

"Yeah…?"

"when did you give it to the CPS?"

"I didn't."

"Then how come the conspiracy count was added? How did they know to do that?"

"I just got a new indictment drafted myself. Gave it to the Prosecutor."

Whelan was shocked.

"You mean the indictment was never signed?"

Lowry looked at Austin and raised his eyebrows. He looked back at Whelan.

"That's right David. Worked though didn't it?"

Whelan fumbled.

"Well, yeah…I suppose…but that invalidates the indictment. And the whole day in fact."

Lowry looked at him and Austin bowed his head.

"Tell you what then David, when *you* are given a case like this, you make sure you dot all the i's and make sure everything is technically sound and above board. Keep getting the case adjourned. Then once you've wasted enough time you can go and organise the funeral."

Whelan was right to speak up. But he was also wrong. Lowry continued.

"What did I tell you yesterday about getting your head out of the textbook?"

"I see what you mean," he said.

"No harm done – no-one's going to notice are they?"

"I suppose not. But it's illegal!"

"There's a choice, David. Little girl, or strict adherence to pointless rules. Which one would make *you* sleep better at night is a matter for your conscience. But only one of the choices means that you're in the right job."

Silence.

"Maybe I am in the wrong job, Sir," said Whelan as he got up to leave the room.

TWENTY FOUR

It was not difficult to find the Calder Pit. Once the helicopter had flown over the Moorfoot Hills and seen the quarry and set of houses there, the pilot was instructed to land just in front of the detached house that stood alone.

Joe Makin had been in constant radio contact with the control room at the station to which he was attached and by the time the helicopter landed, several cars and an ambulance were on their way to meet him there.

He had taken a couple of Officers with him and thought it best to wait for the cars to arrive on the scene – he didn't know who was going to be inside the house and he didn't want to risk being overwhelmed. As long as they were outside, whoever was inside was going to stay there.

Twenty minutes passed. It seemed longer. It always does. It was getting darker now. It wasn't late, but at this time of year dusk tended to set in around 4 o'clock. Makin was struck by the silence. And the glow of the Calder Pit as the sun began setting. No-one spoke. They were all silently imagining what was inside the house that they were standing outside. They were all spaced well apart, so as to ensure anyone slipping out would be seen by at least one of them. And they were all alone with their thoughts. Inside they knew there was a little girl. Whether she was alive or dead was not certain. They had no idea who else was inside. If anyone.

A convoy of armed response units arrived on the scene with an ambulance not far behind. The driver of the ambulance had done well to keep up but, having been told what they had by Makin everyone was fired up and wanted to get to the location as quickly as was safe. Perhaps a little quicker in fact.

There were fifteen officers armed and wearing flak-jackets. They emerged first and made their way towards the house, taking over the spaces occupied by Makin and the other two Officers. They waited for Makin to give the order and once everyone was out of the various cars that arrived he signalled to the Officers nearest the front door to enter the building. They crashed through the front door, though it was in fact not locked. More Officers piled in through the front entrance wihle those at the rear maintained their positions.

The armed Officers inside the building swept through it quickly. They made a cursory search of the open areas on both floors and then, beginning on the second floor, checked every room. There was nothing there except a warm kettle in the kitchen.

They had been inside long enough as far as Makin was concerned. If they hadn't found anyone by now there was no-one there to find. He walked through the front entrance and as he did so he heard "Sir!" coming from a room to his left.

* * *

Hannah had heard a crash. She jumped. The noise had cut almost menacingly into the silence that she had been used to over the last 24 hours. She wriggled around on the floor. Nothing had happened for a few minutes. Then she heard another crash, this time at the door of the cold room. Why was it so loud? Were they angry again? Were they going to hurt her even more this time?

The bangs continued until the door flew open and a light was shone all around the cold room. More lights followed until one came to rest on her. A man dressed in black was pointing something at her but as he came towards her he lowered it and took off his hat.

"Sir!" he shouted.

* * *

Makin entered the cold room and immediately noticed the smell. Even though he was inside the room, for a second he thought the girl was dead and attributed the odour to her decomposing body. But he saw her moving on the floor. And thought to himself that she wouldn't possibly have been dead long enough to create such an overpowering smell anyway. It was a fairly clinical thing to think. But that's what twenty five years dealing with these sorts of things does to you.

He approached her and immediately noticed the rope that was tied behind her. He was overcome suddenly with emotion. That was obvious to the officer who had called him in as he almost violently tried to loosen the rope, emotion driving him.

"It's OK Hannah, we're here to take you back home," he said once he had removed the rope. Her wrists were burned from the tightness of the rope and for a time she struggled to stand.

"Oh God she's freezing – give her your jacket," he said to the officer.

He removed his coat. Hannah even took notice of the fact that that was all he removed.

"Here you go, Hannah, this'll keep you warm," he said with a smile and a tear in his eye. She said nothing.

Makin wrapped the coat around Hannah and she welcomed it without a struggle. As he helped her to push her arms through the sleeves he expected her to wriggle away, try to run off perhaps. But she stayed there, silently co-operating with his efforts to make her feel better.

Makin started to think about the situation outside. The armed Officers were probably still patrolling around the place and wouldn't yet know that Hannah had been found. Makin wanted her in an ambulance as soon as possible and didn't really need her to be faced with a group of men in body armour and carrying rifles as she stepped outside.

"Billy," he said to another of the Officers in the cold room, "go outside will you? Make sure everyone knows we've found her."

"Will do, Sir," replied Billy.

"Oh, and make sure everyone's disarmed. I don't want her scared."

Billy went outside and did as he had been asked. There was no celebration. Everyone knew she was alive. But that didn't always mean that things would stay like that. For all they knew, Hannah was hanging on by a thread. With that in mind, the ambulance crew prepared themselves.

Makin finished putting the coat around Hannah and smiled at her.

"Now, Hannah, this is my friend Alastair," he said, pointing to the owner of Hannah's new coat.

"Hi Hannah," replied Alastair, crouching down and smiling at her. He too was in the same frame of mind as Makin was. Should he crouch down? Should he smile? What would she think? How would it make her feel?

She didn't reply.

"Hannah," said Makin, "Alastair will take you outside to see a friend of ours. A lady. She's going to make sure you're ok. And, you know, she'll probably have a drink and maybe something little to eat for you as well. How's that eh?"

"OK," she said quietly, her head bowed.

Hannah's head was spinning as much, if not more, than

those of the Officers. The next few minutes were going to be strange ones. Because no-one really knew how to treat Hannah. For her own part, she didn't know either. And while Makin would probably never realise it, she would not have gone outside so eagerly were it not for the fact that she was going to be met by a woman. But she did go. And, to show just how unpredictable this situation was, she walked over to Alastair and took his hand, ready to be led outside. He looked at Makin. It was a good job that the cold room was so dark. Both men had tears running down their cheeks.

Alastair took Hannah outside and those that were assembled there looked around at each other with a sense of pride, despair and joy. There were some tears. But everyone knew that there were still jobs to do. Andrea Best, one of the paramedics, walked over to meet her.

"Hi Hannah, I'm Andrea."

Andrea noticed that Hannah's head was still bowed and was not surprised that she received no greeting in return for hers.

"Hannah, do you want to come and sit in our ambulance? I want to make sure you're ok. And, guess what – I've got some juice and biscuits and lollies and all sorts of things you can have!"

Andrea put out her hand for Hannah to take. She was surprised this time. Hannah wouldn't take her hand. Instead she pressed herself into Alastair and would not move. It wasn't clear as to why. There was nothing wrong with what Andrea had said, was there? She wondered. Hannah wasn't talking. And now she was clinging to someone of the same gender as those who had hurt her. There really is no right way to deal with this situation. You just have to be as understanding as you can be. Avoid tears as best you can.

"I'll come with you, Hannah," said Alastair, "It's ok you know. Andrea is a very nice lady. She'll look after you until we can get you home."

A good choice of wording in the circumstances. If going into the ambulance with the lady meant going home then there really was no argument. But Hannah, once in the ambulance, clung to the notion of going home and rejected Andrea's offer of orange juice.

"I want to go home."

"I know you do but we have to take you to the hospital," said Andrea, with a smile.

"No – I want to go home. I don't want to go to a hospital."

"Tell you what, why don't we…"

"NO!!"

"Hey – it's OK!" she said trying to restrain Hannah who was trying to get out of the ambulance.

"Get off!"

She let her go. But she didn't go far. She stood looking, as she had done the day before, at the glow of the Calder Pit. It was still there, waiting for her, red as it was the previous day. She was pleased to see it again. It was not as eerie as yesterday – now it seemed welcoming. She knew that seeing it again meant that she was no longer going to be hurt. She thought about what had happened to her since the last time she had seen it. The hurting, the smell, the cold.

* * *

Joe Makin knew where the smell was coming from after he had shone a torch around for a moment or two. And he really didn't want to open the latch door. He knew he had to. He approached it slowly and wiped his eyes. It wasn't heavy, constructed as it was, in an amateurish way out of cheap wood that was beginning to feel the onset of rot. He shone his torch down through what was now a gap in the floor.

"Oh Jesus no," he said to himself.

Below him were a set of lumps in the ground, around four feet in length. He counted them. Eight. And he knew what they were. The bodies of eight girls probably around Hannah's age.

He looked at the officers who stood behind him still carrying their weapons. When you're used to the concept of this type of discovery, once you accept its plausibility, you are no longer shocked by it. You almost expect it. Sometimes, you prepare yourself for something worse. It's just a matter of experience. No shock. Not nervously excited. Philosophical instead, perhaps. You know it happens. You found out a long time ago. And so you allow yourself a stream of tears as you ask yourself why it keeps happening. You wonder if it will ever stop.

They all knew what had to be done. Nobody spoke until Makin did, a long minute later.

"Start bringing them up please."

He left the cold room, such was the privilege of his position in the force. And he walked out of the house. He saw Hannah standing staring into the distance. Andrea was standing a few metres behind her, as though waiting for her. Everyone else was standing, watching. No-one was talking to her. He walked up to her and crouched down, looking as she did at the Calder Pit. He stayed like that, matching her height, until his legs went numb.

Neither Hannah nor Makin spoke for some time. He didn't want to look directly at her. She would not like that. They both stared out at the Calder pit. Makin wanted to say something. But he had no idea what to say. What do you say to a four year-old girl who has been through that which Makin imagined Hannah had endured?

He felt guilty for being the first person to find her. Like he was trespassing on the rights of her family. She was alive, at least, and while the family would only thank him and not trouble themselves with his perceived encroaching, he could not get the thought out of his head. She needed to be with them now. Not here. Not at the house, looking at the Calder Pit, the last thing she saw before she was hurt.

Perhaps Hannah didn't realise why she was so fascinated by the glow of the pit. Perhaps she did. Could someone so young be capable of self-awareness to that extent? That she was staring at the last thing she saw before being taken into the house? The last thing she could associate with her life before her violations inside the house. Why else did she stare so longingly?

But Hannah was still a four year-old girl. And Makin was of the opinion that it did not matter what he said to her as long as he said something. He just wanted to talk to her. To see if she would talk back. Recently untied and released, she was unlikely to want to speak. But he had to try.

"Do you know why it's red Hannah?"

"No."

"It's just the light of the sun as it sets, bouncing off the rocks. It's a nice colour isn't it?"

"The sun goes to sleep at night, like me."

"That's right – it does," laughed Makin choking back tears that were dying to be let out.

Andrea walked over to Makin and Hannah.

"We really need to get her to hospital," she said fairly forcefully.

"NO! I want to go home!!"

"It's OK Hannah," said Makin.

He got up slowly from his crouched position and put a hand on Hannah's shoulder. Almost immediately he removed it. She was not his to touch. He looked at Andrea.

"I think it might be best to fly her down to Newcastle to be honest. Her family are waiting for her. We've got enough to deal with here anyway," he said as the first body was being brought out.

He turned Hannah away from the house hurriedly so as not to let her see what was happening. He crouched down again.

"You see that?" he said pointing to the helicopter.

"Yeah."

"Do you know what that is?"

"Hellycopter"

"That's right, Hannah. It goes very fast. If you want to, we can go to your house in it right now. I want to meet your mummy and daddy."

She looked at Makin now, tears forming in her eyes but not falling. She shook her head. It was too much. Too early to be trusting those who she had no real reason to doubt. Makin tended to be self-analytical and he now thought about his choice of words. What he said to Hannah had sounded strange to him, like it was something a kidnapper might say. But what else could he say? Perhaps he was being too analytical. There was no other option but to get her into the helicopter. He had to get her home.

Makin cursed himself again, taking his mobile phone out of his coat pocket and dialling a number. He should have had this idea earlier.

"Jim?"

"Yeah?"

"It's Joe Makin."

Lowry was in the Police room. He looked around him as he spoke. Austin sat with his elbows resting on his knees. Looking tired. But looking expectant. Looking up at Lowry, probably trying to assess his face to see if he could work out what was happening. Whelan was back in the room now, having thought about the bigger picture. Alan Riley was standing by the window. He had turned around now too. He wanted to know who was calling. Lowry looked at them all in turn as he began to feel adrenaline rush through his entire body as he realised that now was the time to ask a question of the ultimate significance.

"Oh God Joe, tell me you've found her."

Please.

"We've found her Jim, she's standing here with me now."

It sounded like a cough at first, as Lowry let out a thousand tears. He slid down the wall against which he was resting and did not look at the other men. He gave them a fairly weak thumbs up so as to let them know that Hannah was ok.

"Thank God, Joe," he said as he wept.

Austin was not particularly surprised by Lowry's reaction. His was similar, though not as pronounced. What did surprise him was the reaction of David Whelan. He had learned quite a lesson from this. The rules did not matter at all. Austin rose from his chair and shook Alan Riley by the hand. When he turned to shake Whelan's hand, he saw that Whelan was already well into an episode of tears himself. The fact that the handshake turned into a hug was all the more surprising.

Four big boys, in the Police room at Newcastle Crown Court, all crying. If the public only knew, thought Whelan.

Makin looked down at Hannah and smiled.

"Are the parents anywhere near you?" he asked Lowry.

"No, I'll go upstairs though."

Lowry rushed upstairs, Makin still on the other end of the line. There was no-one outside of the Courtroom. For some reason, Hannah's family were still in Court. Perhaps they were comforted by the official setting. As though being surrounded by professionals gave them a sense of relief. That there was more chance of Hannah being found. Lowry walked in.

It was almost as though he was delivering a verdict. But

no-one needed to hear the words – it was plain from the expression on his face. He looked up at the Judge, along to the Bar and his eyes came to rest on those of Hannah's family.

"She's OK," he said.

Someone cheered. Some people shook hands. Julie and Paul started to cry.

"They are going to fly her down in a helicopter to take her to the hospital. Here, I mean, the RVI. They're about an hour away," he looked to Paul and Julie, "come outside – you can speak to her over the phone."

Lowry received thanks from Paul's brothers and teary nods from Hannah's parents. And he felt like a king.

Julie and Paul were led out of the courtroom by Lowry, who still had his mobile phone in his hand.

"Just wait here a second," he said, as he lifted the phone to his ear.

"Joe?" he asked, wondering if Makin was still there after what was probably a few minutes since he last spoke to him, before having come upstairs to Court.

"Yeah?"

"Good you're still there. I've got Hannah's parents here."

"OK, mate, I'll put her on."

Lowry could feel himself inhale deeply as he momentarily assessed the enormous significance of what he was about to say to the Taylors. This was the first time he had been able to say such a thing. And he smiled from ear to ear as he said it.

"Here you go," he said, looking at Julie and passing her the phone, "someone who wants to have a quick word."

"Hello?" she asked, expecting a Scottish Officer.

"Mummy?" came the reply.

Julie burst into tears.

"Yes, it's mummy," she said, slowly. Such was her emotion, and perhaps even disbelief at first.

Paul could not hear his daughter's voice. Only one person could hold the phone at a time. But it didn't matter all that much. He would see her soon. His reaction was the same as Julie's. He too was overcome. He wrapped his arms around Jim Lowry and thanked him. Lowry reciprocated the customary pats on the back.

"Are we going home now?" asked Hannah.

"Yes we are," said Julie, almost laughing through her tears, "you're coming home very soon."

"I want to go home, mummy."

"I know darling. But you are a long way away you know."

"I am with some doctors and nurses."

"I know you are. They are going to look after you until you go to the hospital."

"I don't want to go there. I want to go home."

"You will, very soon I promise."

"No – now!"

Makin crouched down to Hannah's height once again.

"Is that your mummy, Hannah?"

Hannah nodded.

"Can I speak to her for a moment? I want to ask her a question. Is that ok?"

Hannah slowly passed the phone to Makin, who remained crouched, though it was starting to hurt his legs.

"Mrs Taylor?"

"Yes?"

"It's Joe Makin here, Lothian and Borders Police."

"Oh God thank you so much Mr Makin. You've saved my little girl."

"I just came to the house. You've got Inspector Lowry to thank, not me."

"How is she? Honestly?"

"She is cold and she misses her mum, Mrs Taylor. But

she's been talking, which I always think is a good sign. She wants to come home though, don't you Hannah?"

She nodded.

"How far away are you?"

"Well, see, there's the thing. I arrived here by helicopter. It'll take a good three hours to drive down, but we can fly her down right now. She's just not all that keen on getting in at the moment."

"I'll talk to her."

"OK, here you go."

"Hannah?"

"I want to go home now."

"You are coming home right now. But it's a long way away. I want you to go with Mr Makin in the helicopter. He is going to look after you until you get home."

"I don't like the hellycopter."

"Hannah, it's ok! You'll be fine. Let Mr Makin and the Police men look after you. We are going to wait for you at the hospital."

Hannah sighed. Hospital.

"OK," she said.

"Daddy wants to speak to you first though."

Julie smiled at Paul as she passed him the phone. Perhaps it was just the thrill of having her daughter rescued. Paul returned the smile half-heartedly. He knew it probably didn't represent forgiveness. And if it did, it was a temporary foregiveness.

"Hannah?"

"Daddy I am going in a hellycopter."

Paul was expecting one of several things. Silence. Or perhaps a question to the effect of why she was left beside the car at the supermarket.

"Are you? Wow – that's exciting isn't it? I've never been in a helicopter before"

"It's ok," she said.

Maybe it was the word 'ok' that triggered Paul's question. One he should perhaps not have asked. Or perhaps he should.

"Hannah, are you ok?"

Silence.

Heartbeats.

"Hannah?"

"I'm sore."

She started to well up. But, again, she didn't cry like her parents had been crying.

Paul wished that he hadn't asked the question. He knew what sore meant. And he couldn't think of anything else to say.

"Hannah, go with the Police man and mummy and me will see you at the hospital."

"I know."

"I love you, Hannah."

"I love you as well Daddy."

He managed to say 'bye' before starting to cry again. This was a happy moment. But it was the start of an unhappy time.

★ ★ ★

Makin climbed into the helicopter with Hannah and the two Officers who had come with him. Three men. But Hannah didn't seem to notice that.

"Are you a Police man?" she asked.

"Yes I am, Hannah. These men are from the Police too," he said, pointing them out. They smiled back at her but were lost for words. It didn't matter. Hannah seemed to be more interested in looking out of the window. Makin sat beside her, wrapping a blanket around her. She was initially pleased to be warmer. But then she remembered the car journey up to

Scotland and felt like Makin was about to kiss her on the forehead. She moved away from him and while he didn't understand the specific reason for her doing so he was unsurprised that she did. She was obviously uncomfortable with his proximity and he felt foolish for not realising. He moved across to a seat on the other side of the helicopter.

She had talked. And then had clammed up. Because while she knew for sure that she was being rescued something would suddenly remind her of the three men who had raped her. And she seemed to shun the Officers every time they so much as looked at her. She was too weak to complain about getting into the helicopter. She trusted the Police men. But she was frightened of them. Maybe they were going to hurt her too. They weren't. Were they? Would it always be like this?

She curled up into a ball as she sat in the helicopter. She stared out of the window in silence, watching the glow of the Calder Pit until it was out of sight.

TWENTY FIVE

There was still business to attend to. Simon stood up to address Charles.

"Your Honour, in the light of what has been said in Court, which is a relief to all of us, there is a matter outstanding."

"Yes Mr Silver, I am a man of my word and I am bound by what I said. As such the Defendant...actually I don't suppose I can refer to him as a Defendant any more...can be released."

This was quite a mixture of emotion for the family. Hannah had been found alive. The whole affair was essentially over now – she would be returned to them. But Hopper was a free man. Free to do the same to other children. Their eyes turned to Simon whose embarrassment was hidden from them to the extent that it made him appear nonchalant. Simon Silver was to them the reason why Hannah was not found sooner. What kind of man was he? Someone that would allow a paedophile to wander the streets and take a child? How could he care so little? Was it just more work for him? Another trial fee? Had he not seen us crying? Why did it not affect him?

It did affect him and it always would. They would soon find out just how much.

"Mr Silver there is the small matter of Mr Hopper's whereabouts after release. Earlier today you told me he was intending to leave the area."

"I did, Your Honour, and I anticipated that this may cause concern for the Court. He is, as Your Honour knows, already a convicted sex offender and is subject to registration for at least another three years yet. I have written down his intended address. I ought not, of course, reveal it in open Court so I shall hand it to Your Honour."

And Your Honour can keep it because I have memorised it.

"Mr Silver I will hold onto this if it suits. It can be brought to the attention of those who need it regarding continued registration and need not be said in open Court. Do you have a copy?"

"Your Honour I don't suppose I need one."

"Indeed. I will therefore retain this address and grant Mr Hopper permission to live there for the remainder of his period of registration. If further changes of address are required in the future, these will have to be done more officially, through those instructing you Mr Silver I expect."

"Grateful, Your Honour"

Especially grateful that you kept the piece of paper. Now I am totally backed up.

Simon left Court and went to the cells. The officers already knew about the release but were, at his own request, going to take Hopper back to the prison where he could gather his property and be released from there. He could make his own way from then on.

Hopper turned to Simon.

"Well Mr Silver, may I say that was a sterling performance. I'll use you again!"

He had such a look of content on his face. And that was all he said. The officers took him round to the back door and ushered him onto the prison bus, Simon still standing by the conference cells out of sight. He would go back to prison and collect his belongings. And then he would be free.

He would use him again? Simon now knew that there would be another time. Other times. That Hopper would forever be able to hold him to ransom. Every time he abused a child over the next 30 or 40 years. He owned Simon.

There are times when we accept our fate. We bury our heads through our own inability to effect change. We get on with our lives getting slowly used to the presence of the cloud above us. It's not so bad, it could be worse – it's not like Hopper would hold him to ransom every single day. He would lie low most of the time only to appear when he needed to get out of a situation. Yes, there would be a cloud hanging over Simon for the rest of his career but he would probably get used to it.

There are times when we feel helpless and there are times we feel empowered. There would, as a result of Hopper's release, now be times that other children and other families would be made to undergo the ordeal that Hannah and her family had experienced.

There are also times when we feel our stomach tie in knots, we feel our bodies heat up. We realise the effect of what we are about to do. We realise that we are going to go so far over the line that what we do cannot be undone. And we enjoy both the idea and the feeling that it gives us.

Simon took a piece of paper out of his pocket and wrote on it. He left the cell area, his heart beating so hard he felt it through his robes. Faster and faster. He headed past the family standing on the ground floor and walked towards the lift. Their eyes followed him, this proud saviour of the twisted. They hated him. There was no-one else around the reception area – perhaps their hate could be communicated to him; no-one would see. But they didn't say a word. He looked different this time anyway – something had changed. Was he looking proud? Proud of having set Hopper free? They would have thought so, were it not for the fact that he had spoken to them earlier when Alan Riley had just left the Court without a word. Maybe he wasn't such a terrible person.

He was in no danger. They would not attack him here in the Court building at least. He pushed a button to call the lift.

He waited. The lift arrived and he got in. He turned now to face the family, whose lives had been forever changed for the worse – the family who had no recourse, who had no say in what should happen to Hopper. The family that knew that other children were now in danger from the same man who Simon Silver had helped to liberate. The man who knew the names of the men that had taken Hannah. The man who had forced Simon to mislead the Court and commit a serious offence. A man who would always have that information on Simon, to manipulate him whenever he wanted to. No.

Simon crunched up the piece of paper he had written on and pulled it out of his pocket where he had placed it folded up. As the doors of the lift began to close he looked at the family. He felt his hand tremble. He was about to do it. No-one would know, except the family and they wouldn't ever tell anyone. No good would come of it for them, especially if their actions were to be as Simon predicted. His own actions would go unnoticed, as would the plight of a little girl's life ruined, as unnoticed as a family pushed to the edge of their emotions. As unnoticed as the men who took Hannah. No-one would ever know. As he looked out at the family they could detect a slight smile. He took his hand out of his pocket and threw the piece of paper out through the closing doors. He looked at Paul and nodded to him. He was still shaking. But he was proud of himself now. And he no longer felt held to ransom.

Paul walked up and picked up the piece of paper, straightening it out in his hands and wondering what the hell it was. He began to read it. Just a few short lines of writing.

Information which only three people were supposed to know – William Hopper's new address. Given to them by his Barrister. A link to the three men perhaps? A source of the recourse that the family wanted so desperately? And no-one would ever know how they found him.

EPILOGUE

It was a fairly normal house. It didn't stand out. But they were sure it was the right house. Silver would not have given them a false address – he would have nothing to gain by that at all. In fact he had everything to lose in giving them Hopper's details.

From the look on his face when he threw the paper out of the lift they all knew that Hannah's kidnap must have really got to him. There was no way he would have passed on the information otherwise. They owed him a lot for this. But he had not spoken to them. He had asked for nothing in return. He didn't even know them. How was he to know they wouldn't drop him in it?

The brother had thought about that, discussed it at length on the way down to Nottingham. And they had concluded that it was because Simon was a good man. A simple truth. And he had showed them real trust. He wanted them to have the justice they deserved in the hope that they would do nothing to endanger his own position. But theirs was not the only justice that Simon had sought. Justice, he hoped, awaited the three men that the brothers hoped to find through Hopper.

There is a certain moral code that the brothers knew they would have to adhere to. It meant giving Simon Silver something in return. And when they broke into the house and found Hopper, Paul paid Simon back for taking what he knew must have been a huge risk.

Hopper was startled of course. But he did not appear weakened in any way. He stood up to the brothers in fact. He knew why they were in his house. But they weren't going to see him give in. He was too strong for that.

"How did you find me?" he asked, calmly.

"Easy Hopper, we followed you," said Paul, remembering that Simon needed some degree of protection.

"On the train? I never saw you."

The train? He must have got the train. He certainly wouldn't have had a car waiting for him at the prison. Thanks for the clue.

"That's right, Hopper, we got the same train you did. We kept looking for you, to see where you got off. Can't believe you never noticed us," Paul smiled, "and then we followed you here. And here we all are eh?" he announced, loudly and with his arms outstreched. Not a question. More a declaration of the wondrous predicament in which Hopper would soon find himself.

It never entered Hopper's head that Paul was making it up. It made sense. He must have been followed. Nothing else would explain it. He would never have thought in a million years that Simon had anything to do with it. It would be too far-fetched. It never dawned on him. Paul had done enough to protect Simon now. Given him the thanks that he would perhaps have predicted, but would never be sure of. Paul wondered whether he should make contact with Simon Silver. Perhaps he would. But right now he had other matters to deal with.

"So I suppose you want some addresses then?" Hopper asked.

There was silence. Of course they wanted addresses.

"Not going to happen, boys, sorry," he continued.

Paul stepped aside as his eldest brother Darren stepped forward and swung a short wooden bat coldly into Hopper's face, knocking him to the floor.

It *is* going to happen, Hopper. We've got all night.

The brothers looked around the house, looking for anything with a link to the men. Paper with addresses on, maybe. A computer. A mobile phone. But they knew no names. They couldn't exactly ring all of the numbers Hopper had stored in his phone. Secrecy demanded it. And their own impatience would not tolerate it.

They kept looking anyway. They rifled through pretty much everything in the house. There wasn't much to look through and so they realised that they were getting nowhere after about twenty minutes.

Hopper was still lying on the floor unconscious. Paul noticed that he was in the middle of making a new scrapbook, having searched through one of the bedrooms. He must have already been to some shops and picked up some catalogues. He was acting quickly – he had only been released that morning.

There was nothing particularly sexual in the book. Hopper had already filled several pages with pictures. But they were just pictures of kids modelling clothes with smiles on their faces. Nothing more than that. Paul had never thought about this before – why would he? But he now started to think about how easy it is to find pictures of children. They are everywhere – magazines, catalogues, newspapers, leaflets. We don't notice them. But others do. They amass them. The pictures aren't even remotely sexual. But some people collect them together and use them for their own pleasure. This was not a pleasant reality for Paul. He closed the scrapbook, ripped it up and threw it onto Hopper's bed. It wasn't supposed to symbolise anything. But perhaps it did. Perhaps it showed him contempt. As if to say "I know your secret now and I'm going to put a stop to it".

Hopper regained consciousness after another ten minutes or so. Paul joined his brothers downstairs.

"I found your little scrapbook," he said.

His brothers didn't know what that meant.

"What's this? A scrapbook?"

"Aye, upstairs. Pictures of little kids from magazines."

"Whereabouts upstairs?"

"I've ripped it up now, there's no point looking. You hear that Hopper?" asked Paul, kicking Hopper in the face, "I've ripped your little book up."

The code says that this was Paul's fight and that he should be left alone to do what he needed to do. But his brothers had a few digs themselves. Compared to Hannah, Hopper was getting away more than lightly.

They fired the same question at him, again and again. Hopper refused, for a good long while, to say where the three men were. But he was starting to worry. And it was hurting more and more. After more than two hours he finally gave in. And on the way out, Paul called an ambulance.

Ten days later
Simon Silver sat alone in his living room flicking through the channels as he waited for the Six o'clock News to start. It was still light outside but his curtains were drawn. He hadn't been in to Chambers today. He told them he needed some time off – someone else would cover for him. It would probably only be a matter of pleas and sentences anyway – nothing important, certainly not compared to the case he had done almost two weeks ago now.

Hannah had been saved that same day, ten days ago, but it felt like far longer than that to Simon. He had spent the first week doing pointless small hearings in the Crown Court and had seemed not to care about them at all. That was about the size of it really. Nothing would ever compare to what he had experienced the day Hannah was saved. She haunted him. He had never met her, though he did see her on the news.

He would probably never meet her. Maybe in twenty years she would become a lawyer and he might meet her and apologise to her then. Maybe he would have taken silk by then and could be leading her in a case. Simon's mind had a habit of wandering in this way. That could never happen. In truth, contact with the law was another life decision that had been made for Hannah. There was no way she would ever do this job. It might mean defending people like the three men. They had made her mind up for her in that regard.

But then Simon wondered what he had to apologise about. He had done all he could to save her. It may have taken him a while to decide to make the call to the three men, but that was his only shortcoming. She was saved. Simon told himself that he couldn't go back in time – that what happened was the only plausible thing that could have happened. She had to be taken and she had to be saved. That was the only way that things could have gone, by the very fact that they did. No-one can alter things in that way.

That didn't stop him asking questions. He knew that he had taken a risk that most people in his position would not have been able to justify, hiding as they probably would have, behind protocols and professional conduct rules. It simply wasn't their problem. They would perhaps not have even thought about Hannah beyond the fact that she was an alleged injured party. Simon's mind turned to the words that John Davis had spoken on the morning of Hopper's plea hearing when he had called him a "poor sod". That's how Simon felt. A poor sod who had nobody to talk to about how he felt and what he had done. No-one would ever find out about him passing Hopper's address onto Hannah's family. The family certainly wouldn't want to tell anyone and Simon knew fine well that this was because in doing so they would be setting themselves up for a Court appearance given the fact that when they found Hopper they probably didn't just make polite conversation with him.

The Police, according to the Six o'Clock News, had not disclosed the source as to how they found the three men whose arrests Simon was now watching. While the rest of the country were probably sitting wondering how the Police had been led to them Simon knew that the Police themselves wouldn't even know who their source was. An anonymous call from one of Hannah's relatives after they found out where the men would be from Hopper. Again, they would probably not have found this out by means of mere conversation.

The group's arrogance meant that they had not even thought about setting up alibis. And when none of the three men could explain where they had been on the date of Hannah's kidnap they found themselves charged. An examination of Hannah, gruesome though the concept was, would clarify that those three men were indeed the ones responsible for her kidnap. Which meant that Hopper's plan had totally backfired. Simon sat hoping that they had really made a meal of Hopper. He couldn't be sure but he welcomed the thought of Hannah's father screaming and crying red-faced as he rained down blow after blow onto Hopper.

These were not the thoughts of the classic Barrister. The thought made him feel strong, his emotions running high now. His passion mirrored that of many who he had represented and prosecuted over the years – people defending their homes or sticking up for a friend. Maybe there really is a fine line. But what worried Simon most was that he knew for certain that if he ever saw Hopper again the face that screamed and cried as it beat Hopper would be his own.

The Six O'Clock News moved onto another item and Simon switched off the television. It was still early but Simon would be staying in tonight. He wondered where Hannah would be now. Would she still be in hospital? Maybe she would have gone home by now. Yes, she would be with her family at home ready to start getting over her ordeal. She never would though would she? They never do. Her life was ruined. At four years old. Her years of what should be sexual adventure and discovery would instead act as reminders of what had been done to her. She might never feel close enough to anyone to have a relationship. To have children of her own. And three men who saw her in a car park had done this. They had made that decision. And now they had been found. He wondered who the poor sod who had to represent them would be.

As Simon sat crying his eyes out with the curtains closed he started thinking about the three men and where they would be now. Being interviewed probably. They would hopefully be remanded. And what awaited them on the remand wing Simon knew only too well. They would not be tolerated. Everyone would know their faces. They had been on the news. They would be in the papers. Simon stopped crying for a while. He started to imagine the social justice that would be meted out in prison. It almost pleased him. They deserved to be ripped apart for what they had done. For what they had taken.

But what would Hannah think of that? Would she feel sorry for them? Would she feel bad that she was the reason that they were in prison? The truth was plain to Simon. Yes – she would feel those emotions. That is how much control they still had over her. They would always have that control because a four-year old girl takes what she is given and does not question it. She knows that it is best to please people. She knows not to upset them. She understands that if she is good people will be nicer to her. That is all she understands. She cannot cope with what they had done to her. An adult can process the emotions more easily because they are familiar with the concept of them. But Hannah was not. Her life had been made to take a leap from playing with her friends and getting into trouble for not tidying away her toys to being taken by men she did not know and raped repeatedly. And childhood cannot be juxtaposed with sex. With what only adults understand. Simon began to cry again. Slowly at first. But the more he thought about it the more he began to realise that no punishment would ever be enough. And soon his tears flowed as they had done moments before.

* * *

Paul stood at the kitchen window and looked out into the garden. He could not watch the television. Partly because he was trying to avoid any more reminders of the three men and partly because their arrests came as no surprise to him. They were only found because Paul and his brothers had elicited the information from Hopper. And Hopper had received the force of their emotions towards the three men, such was their frustration that they would never get the chance to get the three men on their own. Hopper was hospitalised after the brothers had been to see him. But he would not say who had put him there because that would lead the three men to find out how they had been found. Hopper had given the brothers their addresses. He had had little choice in the matter of course. He had just wanted to do anything to make them stop – they really went to town on him.

As it turned out, the three men thought that Hopper had set them up anyway. That was unsurprising. No-one would have imagined that Simon had given out Hopper's address. Only he and the family knew that. And it would stay like that. Paul and his brothers had found him and he had directed them to the three men, after a push in the right direction. Hopper was arrested in hospital for eight counts of murder. And there was no way out of it. No-one to use. He would be convicted. There was no doubt. Three men, who thought he had set them up, would surely give evidence against him. He would die in prison and probably not of old age. Paul's attention was not on that now though. He was more focussed at what he was looking at out of the window.

Julie walked into the kitchen and stood beside Paul. She could see that he was crying even though he made efforts to conceal the fact. She stood beside him for a moment, joining him in looking out of the kitchen window into the garden. She looked up at her husband who, though he sensed her gaze, did not look at her. She knew that he probably felt as though she was blaming him for her being taken, which she was, at least to begin with. She hoped she could make amends. She had hardly talked to him since Hannah had gone missing. She had not been there for him – he had no-one to talk to about how devastated he was feeling, being the reason that the men had felt able to seize the chance to snatch Hannah. She realised this now and while she felt punished by his failure to look back at her she took some comfort from the fact that he was holding her hand tightly as his own hand began to shake. He looked down at her. He was crying noticeably now. Paul had only ever cried at the birth of his children. And since then, the only emotions shown in the house had been ones of love. It was a peculiar sight to see Paul cry now. But that did not stop Julie from joining him.

It is one thing for a parent to accept that their grown-up child is having sexual intercourse. But Paul effectively had to accept it now, entirely perverse though this was. Hannah had been exposed to sexual reality; although not of the sort he would have ever prepared himself for. He couldn't get the thought out of his head. He tried to forgive himself for feeling a sense of disgust at Hannah. How could he possibly feel that?

How could she be blamed for being violated? But the thought persisted and accounted for many of his tears. He would never treat her as having done anything wrong – she hadn't. Of course she hadn't! But she seemed almost tainted now. Like she had changed.

She had changed. She would not recover from this. Her life was now defined by what had happened and no amount of quality parenting would change that. In a way she had expertise – no-one in the family would be able to understand completely what had happened. Only she had been there. Only she knew how it had felt. She would probably never want to talk about it and he would probably never want to bring the subject up. And silence on the matter would make the problem fester. The problem was that while Paul knew this, he had no idea how to do anything about it. Maybe each day he would get a little closer to feeling able to talk to Hannah. But he never would.

Julie was more realistic about the issue. She knew that the men would go to trial since they were facing a life sentence even on a guilty plea such was the public outcry at the kidnapping. It would be worth their while having a shot at a trial and they would probably be advised as such by whoever represented them. Julie knew that Hannah would have to talk then. She would be cross-examined. The nightmare would be relived. Counselling had of course been arranged for Hannah and maybe it would help. It hadn't so far. Early days perhaps. But Julie felt that it would only help as far as moving on from what had happened, not strictly repairing the damage that it caused in her subconscious. That would never go away. She would be taught how to forgive the men for what they had done, perverse as it may sound. But this would lead to her being able to associate their acts with them only and not with other people of whom she would be in fear until such time as the forgiveness really took effect.

They both continued to gaze out of the window. Outside on the swing sat Hannah, hardly moving. She clung tightly to one of the chains and stared into space. She was still wearing the jacket given to her by one of the officers who had rescued her. This was her souvenir. The first item that she had associated with release. She had insisted that the officer leave it with her when she was kept in the hospital and he had obliged with a smile that Hannah did not return. Still she sat there. She did not look into the house. She would not return their gaze.

★ ★ ★

Hannah felt cold even though it was a mild night. She had the policeman's jacket around her but still she shivered slightly. She was pale. Her eyes were open but she wasn't looking at anything in particular. She saw the faces of three men. A man who was bigger than the other two, a man whose face was redder than that of the other two and a man who was older than the other two, none of whom had said very much at all. The last time she had sat on this swing had been two weeks ago just before Daniel had started talking about how to get their father to buy them some toys. She tried to remember what she had felt like the last time she sat here but she couldn't. She had little memory now of any feelings before she had been taken. She remembered events of course but not how they had made her feel. All of her feelings were now centred around the car journey, the old house and what had happened inside it. She remembered the darkness of the room she had been placed in. She remembered how it was cold and damp. She could still feel her heart race as it had each time she had heard footsteps approach the door – sometimes they would stop as the door was opened, sometimes they would carry on as the men had merely walked past the door as though she was not there.

What she remembered most though was how she felt the first time they had abused her. How it was so unexpected. How she almost felt like asking them for help even though they were the cause of her need for help. They were the adults though – her only source of assistance. Her source of food. The people she needed to keep from getting angry. She remembered how the first time had seemed longer than the subsequent times. Sometimes they had shouted, other times there was silence. She had been raped nine times by these men.

She remembered how for a whole afternoon she had been left alone, unfed but untouched. She remembered how it felt to anticipate the men coming into the room and how the anticipation grew with every minute that they had remained away from her. The next time that she heard footsteps there were lots of them, the police men and women had found her and she remembered shying away from them at first because she couldn't see who they were. Her eyes used to the dark by then, their torches a sharp affront on her vision. She remembered that they had carried her outside wearing a coat given to her by one of the police men. The coat that she now wore. Then there was a helicopter. A hospital. Her parents. Home.

She looked on. Her head was spinning with the mixture of feelings that she had. She knew that her parents were watching her from the window. She didn't like it. She felt that for the last two weeks she had been constantly watched by people as varied as was their intention towards her. She wished they would leave her to sit alone unwatched. But she also needed to know that they were there. They had not helped her. They had not saved her. For the first time she saw her parents as imperfect people and she was too young to be thinking like this. She had seen them cry. This was not a sight she was comfortable with.

She looks out beyond the confines of the garden now. She

looks out at the people coming and going beyond the fence. She can't see them but she knows they are there. She looks at the adults and the children. She wants to tell them something but she doesn't know how to say it. She wants them to know how she feels. She wants to tell them that there are people in the world who will provide for you and there are people who will take from you. They will take your life away. Most of them already know this to an extent. But not the way she knows it. The way she wants them to know it. She wants them to be careful. She wants them to know that people can do terrible things without warning.

She looks at you, staring quite intently and with purpose. She wants you to understand exactly what happens when a child is taken. She wants you to know that it isn't just a matter of being snatched and attacked, even murdered. She knows that there is more to it than this but she doesn't know the words to describe it. She needs you to know that when these things are done to her she has no idea what they are. She is telling you that she is not ready to be exposed to this reality. She hopes that you won't ignore her but she knows that you probably will. You will want to hide from the knowledge, to tell yourself that it doesn't happen like that. But she is pleading with you to look at why children are murdered and what the purpose was in their having been taken. She is starting to become familiar with the concepts now. She has heard a lot of new words these last weeks. Maybe they shouldn't have told her the words. Maybe they should. She doesn't know yet.

She tells you that the people who hurt her live in secret – people that cannot be tolerated and so exist covertly, to become visible infrequently when opportunity presents itself as her distance from her father in the car park had been. She wants you to know that they liked hurting her – they enjoyed what they did to her. She didn't want to complain, she really didn't.

But it hurt her so much. So she welled up instead. She doesn't want to frighten you – she just wants you to know that what happened to her is something plausible. That she isn't lying. But she has to admit defeat. Hers will not be the message that has any effect because you don't want to accept it yet.

She starts to cry now. For two reasons. One because she is remembering what they did. The other because she is so beaten now, because until the plausibility of what happened to her is accepted then she will not be the last child to suffer in this way. She just wants you to listen. But you won't give her your time. You are disgusted by the sexual nature of what happened and while you feel sorry for the kidnap you don't accept why the kidnap took place. It's not just something people do to cause terror and ruin. That is just a by-product of what is in fact merely preparation for a series of sexual acts. What happens during those sexual acts is unimaginable. It does not sit well with you. You don't want to know about it. Even as she is trying to tell you, you don't want to know and in fact she doesn't blame you for that. You welcome this respite that she gives you. She has forgiven you for your fear. Hide behind it.

A tear runs down her cheek. It burns her face. She has not cried for two weeks. She bows her head. She is sorry if she upset you. She didn't mean to. Don't despise her.

Look away now. She doesn't want you to see her cry. She wouldn't dare impose upon you like that.

END